Jo

Death Gone Wildly Wrong

A Speculative Fiction and
late 20th Century Historical Novel

Bryan Costales

Published by

Fool Church Media
Eugene, Oregon

This novel is a work of fiction. Names, characters, places and incidents either are the product of the author's imagination or are used fictitiously. Other than well known historical people or events, any resemblance to actual persons, living or dead, events or locales is entirely coincidental.

Jo
Copyright © 2014 Bryan Costales

1st Edition 2014: Bryan Costales
2nd Edition 2017: Fool Church Media
Cover Art by Bryan Costales

Softcover ISBN: 978-1-945232-13-8
Epub ISBN: 978-1-945232-14-5
PDF ISBN: 978-1-945232-15-2
HTML ISBN: 978-1-945232-16-9
Kindle ISBN: 978-1-945232-17-6

Manufactured/Printed in the United States of America

Table Of Contents

To

Hannah Gloria

Acknowledgments

This book would not have been possible without wife Terry's sharp eyes for spotting my many nearly invisible mistakes. Various instructors at the San Francisco Writing Salon and the San Francisco Writers grotto have, at moments, steered me in the right direction, making this novel all be better for their efforts.

Others helped in small but significant ways. Gypsy, my dog, for her unwavering companionship. George Jansen for demonstrating that the writing of a novel was possible. And a three star review on Amazon, by William Jeffson III, that clued me into how to make the book more readable.

Part 1

The Early Years

Events of 1998
Joe Bailey
His Final Written Work

I stood at my front window, with its view of the road, and grey cloud-shrouded mountains beyond, and wondered if the snow outside would ever cease to fall. Piled a foot high already, it fell in huge flakes that swirled and danced like fierce fairies. The cold from the glass bit my face.

I was about to brave that cold to fetch my mail when my vision changed —as had become habit in my life. But instead of someone else about to die, I saw my future self. I stood at the kitchen sink and laid out a trout for dinner. Beyond me, through those future kitchen windows was sunlight and a bright blue sky. My body, from behind, turned into a glass-like cutout of myself. I knew in that moment that I would die soon, perhaps within the week.

Oddly I felt relief. You see I had always wondered if I could foresee my own death. But I had waited so long that I had recently begun to suspect my own death might be the exception. I watched my cutout put his hands to either side of his head, as if in surprise, and then the cutout collapsed to the floor and turned whole again. Evidently I will die before I hit the floor.

My vision changed again. A jar with a brain, that floated in clear liquid, was set on a formal pedestal carved from dark wood with gold leaf designs. In the center of a somber multi-tiered circular room, two men walked in, one wore a tattered yellow robe and the other a nondescript brown suit. The man in the robe said, "Jo Bailey's brain." That man's face looked familiar but I couldn't place him. But he was clearly a priest with the Church of Jo which must certainly mean that after my death the church should have my brain, and perhaps my whole body.

And then my vision changed again. A young woman knelt in rain-soaked grass. She leaned forward and used the palm of her hand to wipe a thin layer of rain off the face of a gravestone. My gravestone, with three words below my name, "Founder, Prophet, Father." Mist-like rain fell a little harder. Cold water dripped off her hand. The silence of soft rainfall on grass. She sighed and said, "Perhaps my own life is the sign. I'm still alive Dad, and perhaps that is significance enough."

She touched my gravestone again. I realized she must be Joy, the daughter I never met.

Someone walked up behind her. She stood and turned. That same priest from the room with the brain stood there alongside a stranger dressed in a dark suit and overcoat. Both held identical yellow umbrellas overhead.

Joy wiped rain from her face.

The priest offered Joy his umbrella with a gesture, but she shook her head, so he introduced the stranger, "Agent Robles with the FBI. He's the one who hand-cuffed me back in Gilroy before we flew up north to free Jo. He has some news to tell you."

I recognized the priest then. Ace Hoklins was the man I had asked to become the first founder of the Church of Jo.

Agent Robles cleared his throat and said, "We arrested the two men that blew up your church. They're in custody and will be tried for murder."

Father Hoklins added, "George Wriggles and Larry Yonkers. These are the last two from the Defoe Scallody gang."

Joy studied the FBI man. "Will that leave us safe?" she asked him.

He glanced at Father Hoklins then back at Joy. "Not exactly," he said. The sound of his voice became deeper as he became serious.

"What do you mean?"

"Well there's a lot of chatter about your church. Seems your Jo Bailey made a lot of people angry. I'm glad to see you beefed up the fence around your church. Still I'd be extra careful if I were you."

"How much more careful?" Joy frowned.

Agent Robles crossed his arms and appeared to appraise Joy carefully. "I probably shouldn't suggest anything so expensive, but you might want build a safe room. Someplace armored where you and your employees would be safe from an attack."

At that moment my visions ended and I was back in my home. I wondered briefly why I didn't see a baby afterward. But because that wasn't always the rule, I shrugged.

Perhaps I finally came full circle because the next night I was visited by my ghost. A scratch on the front porch made me curious and, as I approached, I smelled strawberries. I opened the door and my ghost stood not more than a foot away from me.

"Esther," I said. She glowed and was transparent and indistinct.

"I forgive you," she said so softly I might not have actually heard her.

That was all. And then I sneezed and she was gone.

"Thank you," I said and I felt all the tension drain from by body. I had never slept so deeply and comfortably as I did that night.

Events of 1963
Bonnie Wikkens

A letter discovered by her oldest daughter six months after Bonnie's death of cancer.

God how I miss Jo. I only knew him as a boy of course, but long afterward I fantasize him as a man. Jo told me he foresaw his mother's death. That's right. He said he had an image in his head of her as she was shot. So he left school early to run home. But he got home too late. His mother was already dead. Shot to death as he had foreseen. Jo was a weird but sweet kid.

I suppose he seemed sweet because he was so shy, tall with brown hair, great eyes and skinny because he was always moved, never remained still. But he seemed weird to me too because of the things he confided in me.

He told me several times, "I should have run home right away to save my mom. Instead I waited all through recess before I dared to cut class and run home."

Only once did he describe to me what he actually saw. He made me promise to never tell our foster parents or the other kids. I had to cross my heart and pinkie swear before he would tell me. And then he made me walk with him to Meadow Homes Park where our street ended so the other kids couldn't hear. We sat on opposite sides of a green painted picnic table. A breeze made his hair move like a boy prince.

Jo leaned forward, arms crossed, dressed in one of his plaid shirts, and told me seriously:

"I was sat in class when my school room faded away. I was half in school and half in my kitchen at home, you know, like an hallucination but more real."

A big Irish Setter bounded across wide, green grass, so green then that I would later call that color Kodachrome green. Jo paused until I looked back at him. He smiled at me when I made eye contact again. That was when I first thought I was in love with him.

"I witnessed my mother," he continued. "As if I was a ghost in the kitchen. I could only watch. My mom stood at the sink and washed dishes and hummed a soft song; I think 'The Glow Worm' song. I distinctly smelled a rhubarb pie in the oven."

Jo was a sucker for rhubarb pies, but nobody else liked them so he could only have one on his birthday. I baked one for his last birthday because our foster mom didn't know how. Or maybe I had begged her to let me bake that pie. I don't remember which.

"Our front door closed," Jo continued. "My mom heard that sound too. 'Jo', she shouted. But I wasn't really there, some other man was there instead. He was tall and lanky with thick dark hair; he wore slacks and a plain white dress shirt. My Mom turned to look at him and as she turned she flattened into a glass-like flat image of herself. Her image-face looked surprised and as if my mom recognized the man. The pistol in the man's hand looked too big for him and shook in his hands. He shot at her five times, wildly. He missed some, broke the window behind her with another, and hit her only once in her chest. The room reeked of gun powder. She fell to her knees then looked up at him. He said, 'For my dad.' He stepped forward, pressed the barrel of the pistol against her head and shot her one last time in her forehead right between her eyes. As she fell backward she became whole again, no longer flat, but dead."

You have to understand, Jo didn't describe her death in a morbid way. He sounded sad or maybe frustrated. I felt sorry for him so I put my hand on his, and he let me. His hand felt strong.

"What I told you is a secret," he said.

"I know," I told him. "I love you."

He pulled his hand away from mine and said, "You're a great foster sister. But remember it's a secret."

I wanted to hold his hand as we walked back but I was afraid to reach. I worried that if I took his hand again, he would pull free again.

After that meeting he told me again, "If I had only gone home sooner I could have saved her." He must have told me that five-dozen times, and always in private, as if meant to be our secret. And every time soft and close so that I could feel his warm breath.

Well girls, you have the background for my most exciting, frustrating, sad, and memorable camping trip ever, at least until Penny was almost eaten by that brown bear. But you all already know that story, don't you?

Events of 1966
Neil Allen Fitzpatrick, Ph.D.

"My Years Of Protest" (unpublished) the Chapter titled, "Fun and Games with Jo Bailey." Written while he was still in graduate school at the University of California at Berkeley

One student raised his hand and tried to debate the Teaching Assistant. "How can you be sure we all will fail?" he asked from behind me. Curious, I glanced back. He was a skinny kid with short brown hair and thoughtful eyes.

Roger, the TA, crossed his arms and frowned. "You already failed your written entrance exam, which put you in my class. You're first lesson will demonstrate to me how well you think, and how well you can compose and how well you convey those thoughts. Your first exam will provide me with your individual baseline, so that I can measure your progress through my class."

The skinny student raised his hand again. "But shouldn't you grade on a curve."

Roger chuckled. "No. You will all fail."

I suspected that one skinny student might be more than a sheep.

After class, I caught up with that skinny kid and introduced myself, "I'm Neil," I said to him. "Mind if I walk with you?"

"Jo, spelled J O," he said, and shook my hand. Then he looked at me as if he recognized me. "Hey," he said. "I notice you took notes in class, and they didn't seem like they were Melville related."

"My given name is Neil Fitzpatrick," I said. "But most folks call me Raz because of the raz-ma-taz way I play chess."

"Jo Bailey," Jo said. "If you don't mind my asking, what were you writing?"

"Free speech."

Jo waited for me. I gathered he felt I needed to say more.

But to me, an expression like "free speech," back then, was like "plastics" in that movie which came out later called The Graduate. A phrase that contained within itself all necessary meaning.

"Walk with me," I said, and set off at a determined pace toward Sather Gate. "I guess you haven't kept up with events, have you? The Dean of Students ruled yesterday that all those so-called political tables would have to be removed. And that reeks of a violation of our free speech rights."

"You mean all those tables by the Student Union building?"

We crossed over Strawberry Creek's wide bridge and then passed through Sather gate, with its ornate green, aged copper and detailed arches that curved high between multiple tall granite pillars.

Jo stopped in his tracks. "They're gone. All the tables and signs are gone."

"Sheep" I said to Jo. "The students won't do a damn thing."

"But," he began.

I held up my hand. I had a coil of rope in my satchel that I planned to use for a clothesline at home. Thin rope actually, more like thick twine. I had an idea. "An object lesson," I told him. "Take the end and stand over there at that side."

Sather Gate was one wide archway flanked by two narrower arches, and marked where original University grounds ended. Sather Gate stood at one end of a bridge over Strawberry Creek, where the ground was flat and wide, as wide as a two-lane highway. The bell in the Campanile behind us gonged eleven and I could feel the usual cool fog that had piled against nearby Oakland hills. Sadly the fog had finally started to burn off.

He moved over a few steps further toward the left-most edge of the smaller gate. "Far enough?"

"That's fine. Just hold the rope firmly about waist high." I began to feed out rope as I moved slowly backward away from him toward the other side of Sather Gate. As I fed rope, I tried to keep the tension constant I noticed its shadow at first sharp, then blurred because fog evaporated unevenly overhead.

Last summer I had seen another student perform the same trick. I had been amazed then by what I had seen. As I played out my rope, students crossed through the gate. They all moved over behind me to pass. Even where that open end narrowed to a few feet, students still only passed through the opening. Nobody, not a soul, tried to duck under that rope or step over.

I gathered up my rope and went back to Jo. "You see," I explained. I plucked my rope from his hand. "Students are sheep. They can ban tables and keep them away for as long as they want, but students will never lift a finger."

"Wow, I never thought of that." Joe said.

"I'm on my way to join some TAs who want to pen a letter to the Regents. You want to join me?"

Jo then stopped and said something odd, "I can't save anyone. No matter how much I try."

I stopped too and waited for Jo to continue.

"You know," Jo hesitated. "I really need to study. I signed up for a heavy load and all I can do is struggle to keep up with my assignments. I hope you don't mind, but I think I'll head back to my dorm and start Moby Dick."

"Yeah," I said. "I mean, that's why you're in school." I stuck out my hand. "If you change your mind catch me in class."

Jo shook my hand, a firm shake.

I turned away from him and strode off toward Telegraph Avenue, without a glance back. I thought about Jo's comment and couldn't imagine a willow tree boy like that could ever save anyone.

Jo wasn't much to look at back then. But that first day, I'd seen something in his eyes that puzzled and intrigued me. I didn't know then about the many deaths he had seen, but that was why his eyes always seem so sadly understanding.

The next week arrived and Jo was one of the last to sit in class. I sat near the back, self conscious about my new, short haircut. Cut short so the UC Regents would take me seriously when they were forced to negotiate. I watched Jo. He yawned. I supposed he was tired because he'd worked on Moby Dick all night. That made me feel vaguely superior.

The TA stepped into the room, stopped and put his fists on his hips. To me the TA, in that moment, looked like a young man hankering for a fight.

"What are you all doing in class?" he glared at us. His beard was full, his eyes were bright. "Don't you know there's a protest going on? You shouldn't be in class," The TA raised his hand and shook his fist. "You should be out there, out in the quad, fighting for free speech!" He turned and left. A stunned and quiet class-room remained in his wake.

I was as surprised as everyone else. I had never thought Free Speech would become a movement. One by one the other students got up and left. Jo waited until nearly last. He dropped his essay on Roger's desk. And, after he left, I noticed students behind him also began to drop their essays on the desk to form a small pile atop Jo's essay. Sheep, I thought. They're all sheep.

I followed Jo out.

Events of 1998
Joe Bailey
His Final Written Work

After I witnessed that image of my death, I continued to stand at the window. Outside the snow began to fall harder. I could barely see my mailbox, two steps outside my front door. I turned and faced the inside of my home, a modest place to live at the end. A propane fed fireplace crackled with fake metal logs. A book shelf filled with books only a few of which I had taken the time to read. My home was filled with the aroma of chili. I decided to make corn bread with my last package of Jiffy.

You see, I knew I would be reborn into the next dimension, so I didn't fear death. I only regretted that I had so little time to wrap up loose ends. Next to me on the kitchen table —two days after my vision— I have begun a list. How my life ended, is one check-mark on that growing list. On that list are the profound, such as my one and only letter to my daughter, and another letter to tell the Church of Jo they must have my body. Other checked items are more routine: Cancel my subscription to Harper's Magazine; and bequeath my stove to my neighbor Annie Proulx.

To understand how my life ended, you have to understand how my life began. I was named Jo because the doctor's pen ran out of ink. He had written down the "Jo" of "Joe" and shook his pen to get the ink to flow again when my mother said, "Jo it is. Two letters. I like that." Or at least that's the story my mother told me when I was much younger. From my birth in that hospital in Concord, California to my death in

Centennial, Wyoming, my life has followed a tortured, twisted and convoluted path.

I see my life as a pinball game. Not one of the new ones with electronic displays and only three balls, but the old kind with lots of bells and incandescent lights, a huge death head whose eyes displayed the score and with five balls to play, like the five lives of Jo Bailey. You can hope to win bonus balls, of course, but I never won any.

With my first pull of the plunger, my first ball let fly, and my life started as a young boy at home who imagined he witnessed people die. My abusive father beat my mother and tortured me, then moved away only to die of a heart attack. My crazy mother took me to a quack doctor and had my head drilled to let out the evil spirits. That life ended when my mother was murdered. Afterward I was taken away and placed with my first foster family. The ball missed the flippers and was swallowed down the center when Ester died at PG&E camp.

My second pull of the plunger launched me into college and the draft. During my second ball I first realized that, although I could predict death, I could never prevent anyone's death.

A third ball rushed up the channel: past marriage; past my wife dead of cancer; past my only trip to Europe; past publication of my first book. That ball racked up millions of points.

The fourth ball hit a bumper lit red with a devil face and caused me to get shot at while speaking at the Greek Theater, shot at again in the Mojave Desert, and kidnapped from in front of my armored house in San Francisco.

Which brings me to my fifth an final ball. Hidden in the folds of my coat. The only way I could be safe was to disappear completely. I threw that ball toward the Philippines while I skulked away to hide in Wyoming. But I have finally seen my death, and that ball has finally rolled back to the shores of the old U.S. where others will continue to play that ball, I am certain, long after I die.

I was Jo Bailey.

Events of 1963
Bonnie Wikkens

A letter discovered by her oldest daughter six months
after Bonnie's death of cancer.

Our fateful PG&E camp trip began early Saturday morning, like all our summer trips did, after sun-
rise and after breakfast. Still half asleep we all piled
into our family's old, pale blue Packard Clipper station
wagon with its outrageous tail fins and luggage tied on
top with too many loops of manila rope. Jo got a window seat because he was oldest. I sat opposite Jo
because I was second oldest. I needed a window seat
too because our car smelled bad, like mildew from
sodas and things that had spilled during our many
trips to school and shopping. I always rode with my
window cracked a little for fresh air.

Jo liked to ride with his window fully rolled
down. Boys! He flew his hand in a wind made by the
car's movement. But when we hit open road, Jo had to
roll his window up because younger kids seated behind
him complained. You see, that old car had three rows
of seats!

Our foster-mom was Susan. She always wore
floppy cloth hats in summer, practical but an old fash-
ioned style, colorful with silk flowers around the brim. I
can picture her, the way she lifted her hat and brushed
away her long blond hair to talk to us. "Jo," she said,
without a glance back. "We signed you up for canoe lessons."

"Canoe lessons...." Jo said. He put his hands
over his face and moaned, "Oh no...."

Jo didn't like new things. He was crack smart at
English, writing and chess, but didn't much like sports

and never liked to learn anything physical. He complained when PE class made him learn to swim. He hated the thought of canoeing. But like all things he tried and hated, he quickly became an expert.

We arrived at camp in late morning. By that first afternoon I lay on a swim platform that floated part way out into the lake. Sunlight played hide and seek among white fluffy clouds. My private platform was perhaps twelve feet square. I wanted to get a good tan and the sun was just high enough. I lay on my back on my damp towel over cool wooden planks, watched one fluffy cloud and imagined animals or cartoons. I wore my first two-piece suit and I felt sexy. Or as sexy as I could feel at that age. My suit bottom was probably more like a modest skirt.

After a while an instructor in a canoe and eight other canoes arrived two kids in each canoe, all wearing old-fashioned brown cork life vests. I sat up to listen. I could sit cross-legged then, when I was young. I need a chair these days, although, I'll never go camping again.

I sat up and noticed Jo seated in a nearby canoe. I sat up and wrapped my arms around my legs because he wasn't alone. He sat behind a red-haired girl. I noticed he looked at her, he didn't look at me. Right away I didn't like her. Maybe her pale skin put me off — you know how much I like to tan and how much I didn't like you girls to lose your summer tans in winter. Or maybe I found her freckles ugly. They ran all over her face and down her arms like brown snow.

Kids in turn, each said his or her name and I learned that girl's name was Esther.

Jo looked at her and asked, "Like sweet esters off a fine perfume?"

She smiled at him which made me sick. "No silly, like an Esther egg," she said, and they both laughed.

Jo, I clearly see, liked Esther. I imagine that her dimples enchanted him and she smiled at him whenever he said anything. Or maybe her clever way with words. Or maybe she was new.

I was disappointed of course but tried to not reveal how I felt. I was so warm and comfy on that swim platform that I stretched out my legs again and wiggled my toes and listened.

Esther turned out to be a sophomore same as Jo. She pronounced her R's in an odd way so Jo asked, "Where are you from?"

"I was born in Baton Rouge, Louisiana and went to school there until last year. Then we moved to Redding because my Dad changed jobs. He started to work for PG&E. You know what Baton Rouge means, don't you? That means red stick."

She said red stick wrapped in a sugary sweet voice that made me want to gag. But they both laughed again. I felt my hair itch so I scratched my head.

I could see that Jo felt comfortable with her. You have to understand, Jo never felt comfortable with girls even me. Not as a girl anyway. Not yet. Still, I could tell he was a little self-conscious about how he looked. His nose was covered with white zinc oxide, and he hated his swim trunks with a flower on his left pocket. But Esther didn't appear to notice.

Flowers were a hobby of our foster mom Susan. My swim suits were always an explosion of flowers, never plain. Back in our foster home our bathroom was all flowered too. Toilet cover, rugs, towels, everything and explosion of bright flowers. And all curtains in all rooms were flowered with large daisy prints. So you see, Jo got off easy with a single flower on his pocket.

The canoe lessons looked fun at first and I watched as all those kids paddled out and around my swim platform. At first they collided with each other which reminded me of bumper cars. After ten minutes or so of chaos, the instructor finally taught them how to turn their canoes and how to go straight and how to stop they could run into each other.

After what seemed to like too long, the instructor told them to all form into a circle around him. I watched from my platform. I was hot under that bright sunshine and I had forgotten to wear a hat. They all listened to the instructor, so I shaded my eyes with my hand and listened too.

The instructor was a young man with brown hair and a brown moustache. One of those handlebar moustaches like in old Westerns. He finally introduced himself. "Hi," he said. "I'm Freddy."

Several of the kids said in unison, "Hi Freddy."

"Pay attention. These canoes are safe provided you never, and I mean never, stand up in one. If you fool around and do fall out, swim to shore right away, never try to get back into your canoe. And don't hang onto your canoe, because the water is still winter cold and can quickly make you unconscious if you don't get out right away."

Freddy held up his hand and made a V with two fingers. "Number two," he said. "Only paddle close to shore. Never go out too far. You see the swim platform." He pointed at my swim platform where I sat.

Jo looked. They all looked. I waved at Jo. He may have smiled back.

"Never," Freddy told them, and then again for emphasis, "Never paddle further from shore than the swim platform. That's about how far healthy young kids like you can swim."

I looked from my platform to shore. The distance didn't appear that far. I had already dog-paddled that far and I knew Jo was a strong swimmer.

"That seems far," Esther said.

"You're wearing a float vest," Jo pointed out. "With that you can dog-paddle to shore easy."

I watched Ester smile at Jo again. Joe smiled back at her. I found I liked her less and less.

"Okay kids," Freddy said. "Have fun paddling. Just be sure to be back in two hours for dinner."

Seven canoes jockeyed around and headed diagonally toward shore and away from camp. I watched Jo. He looked around and noticed something behind them. "Let's go that way," he said to Esther, and pointed back along shore.

"Okay," Esther said. She started to paddle her end to turn.

"Smart move," Freddy said to them.

I fumed at that remark because I thought he said Jo was smart to go off with that other girl. But then he went on and I realized he meant something else.

"If you walk up-creek from that inlet you'll find a beaver dam."

"Cool," Jo said. And "Thanks," to Freddy.

I stood and watched them paddle off toward that inlet. Ester behind watched Jo so when his paddle moved to the opposite side she moved her paddle too. Ripples formed a V as they paddled away from me.

I hitched a ride back with Freddy because I didn't want to swim again. When I swam out earlier I had experienced a layer of frigid water less than a foot below that summer-warm surface. Cold water grabbed at my legs and tummy. I really didn't want to swim on top of that ice cold, under-layer again.

Events of 1966
Neil Allen Fitzpatrick, Ph.D.

"My Years Of Protest" (unpublished) the Chapter titled, "Fun and Games with Jo Bailey." Written while he was still in graduate school at the University of California at Berkeley

I continued to follow Jo as he walked toward Sather Gate while other students ran in that same direction past him. Ahead of him and through the gate. A huge crowd had formed in the wide plaza between Sproul Hall and the Student Union Building. A single police car was parked, central to all, surrounded by hundreds of students, maybe a thousand or more.

I followed Jo until we both felt the crowd push us along. First one person then another got on top of that police car and yelled and gesticulated toward the crowd. Spontaneous chants of "Release him. Release him," punctuated those speeches.

Jo started to wander his way inward toward the police car. Eventually he stood nearby and peered around at the crowd. His eyes swept right past me without recognition. Credit (or blame) to my hair cut. I moved closer and stood a few people away from him.

Jo bent and looked inside the car. I bent and looked too. A wildly hairy older student, probably a grad student, sat next to a uniformed cop in the back seat.

"Who are you?" Jo ask the hairy man.

The grad student looked at him and said simply, "I'm Jack Weinberg."

"How come you're under arrest?"

"They arrested me because I want to protect the right of students like you, to protest freely."

22

"But I don't protest," Jo said.

Jack shook his head and laughed. "You will," he said. "You will."

"I have your food," a young mans voice said close by, so Jo straightened and stepped away from the car. A young man handed Jack a sandwich and a carton of milk through the car's window.

Jo looked around and spotted me. At last! I waved to him and gestured for him to follow me over toward the steps of Sproul Hall.

From higher up on Sproul Hall's steps we watched the protest unfold. Another grad student with short curly blond hair was escorted through the crowd toward the car. He stopped next to the hood of the police car and took off his shoes. Then he climbed on the police car and waved his arms for quiet.

As the grad student began to speak, I watched Jo and he was immediately captivated. Then I too turned to watch.

"There's a time," the man began, then paused for quiet. "There's a time when the operations of the machine becomes so odious, makes you so sick at heart, that you can't take part. You can't even passively take part."

"Who is that?" Jo whispered to me.

"That's Mario Savio," I said. I couldn't take my eyes off Mario.

"And you've got to put your bodies upon the gears and upon the wheels, upon the levers, upon all the apparatus, and you've got to indicate to the people who own it that unless you're free, the machines will be prevented from working at all."

The crowd let out a roar of approval. Jo and I were jostled backward toward the building as others pushed ahead of us.

"Jo," I said. "Looks like whether you like it or not, you're part of a protest."

"I like it," he said, then added, "I hope protesting won't hurt my grades."

Events of 1963
Bonnie Wikkens

A letter discovered by her oldest daughter six months
after Bonnie's death of cancer.

Outside my hospital window I watched a blackbird perched on the bare limbs of late autumn. He
looks around at a world that must be much too large
for him to comprehend. He reminds me of myself as I
face the unknown and unknowable that exists afterward. I feel as small as that blackbird, except, as he
flew off, I could see he was totally free of pain.

Next afternoon, in camp crafts class, I made a
pair of moccasins. Just like from a hobby store with a
pattern already cut out with holes so all I had to do was
lace up with leather strips. I knotted a scratchy acorn
to the front of each. They looked like fashion moccasins, like you might find in a fancy store, or so I imagined.

I walked around in my new, slightly too-big moccasins and looked for Jo, but he didn't seem to be anywhere, so I decided to go find that beaver dam myself. I
didn't use a canoe, instead I walked across and
through dry sparse woods. When I arrived, the stream
was hot and quiet. Just a buzz of insects and a rat-tat-
tat of one distant woodpecker. I couldn't find any beaver dam or even anything that might be a beaver dam. I
was about to give up and head back when voices came
up-creek toward me. I was certain one of the voices was
Jo's so I hid.

I hunkered down on a patch of sand behind a big
fallen tree stump and waited for them. You have to

25

remember I was still a young girl back then, and found it easier to hide than to confront, or so I thought. Besides, I couldn't run or they'd spot me. That sand turned out to be soft and warm and felt much better than the rocks.

Jo and Esther walked into view and stopped. I watched them listen like I had. They must have felt hot and uncomfortable, exposed like that on loose gravel. Esther was dressed in a pale-yellow summer frock which I was glad to see clashed with her red hair. Jo wore a blue PG&E tee-shirt tucked into blue denim jeans. They both wore white tennis shoes which made me feel a bit superior with my hand-made moccasins.

Esther took Jo's hand. "Let's go over there," she said, and pointed at a cluster of pine trees on the side opposite me. "We'll be cooler under those trees."

Jo smiled at her and let her pull him toward shade. I notice he didn't pull his hand free of hers like he had with me. I shifted quietly so they wouldn't see me. Jo looked happy and lucky and proud. I despised Esther because she could make Jo feel that way.

They sat on a shaded log parallel to the creek border. Their feet still in tennis shoes rested in shallow water.

I wished I could have shown myself so I could soak my feet too, but to show myself would have broken that mood. And I would have been embarrassed no end. So I suffered in heat, and drew my satisfaction from spying.

Jo looked around. "I smell strawberries," he said. That was such an odd thing to say out there that I remember distinctly.

"That's my lipstick," Esther told him. "Strawberry flavored." She smiled at him and then sat up straight and looked idly around.

They sat quietly for a moment. Esther's yellow dress contrasted with Jo's blue tee-shirt and jeans. They sat slightly apart. That pleased me.

"Do you want to kiss me?" Esther asked, which broke my mood. She was looking straight ahead, not at Jo, but at me as if she had asked me. I wanted to say, "No no," but remained quiet, afraid to speak.

"Um," Jo mumbled. "Yeah." He looked at her.

Esther closed her eyes then turned her head to face Jo. Her pink lips puckered.

I didn't want to watch, but I watched anyway. I've seen you girls watch too, like at scary movies. You'd cover your eyes to avoid something gruesome, but peek through your fingers and watch anyway. Why do girls do that but boys don't? I always wondered that.

Jo acted inexperienced and clumsy and he struck me as afraid he'd miss. He kept his eyes open. He kissed her briefly on her lips, then he sneezed.

I had to cover my mouth to not laugh. I knew about Jo's allergy to strawberries. He couldn't eat them, not ever, or even have strawberry flavored ice cream. His throat would close up and he would gasp for air. That happened once at dinner and our foster-dad William had to drive him to the hospital emergency room.

"Was I that bad?" Esther opened her eyes and glared at him. Her chin jutted out, as I recall, adult like.

"Sorry," Jo said, and coughed. "I'm allergic to strawberries." He sounded hoarse. "A good kiss," he said. "Yes."

Ester smiled at Jo. "Good. In that case we can try again tonight. After dinner."

"Don't we have to stay in our cabins after dark?"

Esther draped her arm over his shoulder, pal-like and conspiratorially. "We'll sneak out," she pretend-whispered in his ear.

Sneak out? Why didn't I think of that? I was surprised. I guess I was too damned honest as a kid. A few more years had to pass before I learned to lie.

Esther kissed him a light peck on his cheek. "I'll arrange everything." she said in low tones. Then she jumped up, ran out into bright sun and stood mid-creek ankle deep and waited for Jo with her hands planted firmly on her hips.

Jo watched her and used the back of his arm to rubbed his nose.

"Coming?" Esther asked.

Jo stood and walked up to her and sneezed once again.

I watched them walk away. They kicked water at each other and Jo threw stones at trees. They didn't try to kiss again and that was really okay with me.

Events of 1970
John Mellion, PFC U.S. Army

Transcript from an audio tape sent to his parents after his death.

Hi Dad. Hi Mom. The weather in Viet Nam stinks. I mean really smells bad. You know, lots of rotten smells of leaves and fruit, like the smell of fertilizer only worse. And rain falls in buckets. No, don't think hard rain. I mean empty a full bucket over your head and you'll get the idea. Rain all last night and this morning is hot as hell and humid.

[Loud rock music in the background]

Hey, turn that crap down. I'm making a tape.

[Music fades]

You remember, I told you in my last tape about that fellow Axel Winslow who was from northern California too. Well he died last week. He was patrol and was blown up by a hand grenade tossed at him by a woman in a village. The woman carried a baby wrapped in a cloth and pulled the hand grenade from the baby's wrap. Wasn't a real baby of course. Sometimes they try to look pregnant and pull a hand grenade or a gun from their fake bellies. That's the war we fight. Say hi to Mom for me.

[Laughs]

On days when I stay here on leave, other guys will hand me, or one of the other guys in our outfit, letters. You know, letters to wives or children or parents. They say, "Please mail this for me if I don't come back."

Most come back but some don't. Those that come back ask for the letter back. Those that don't come back. Well I mail the letter for them. Nothing else I can do.

[A man's voice says, "Tell them about Sammy."]

Yeah. Sammy was really young. You have to be sixteen to enlist and if you're that young you parents have to sign. Well Sammy was fifteen. We don't know how he got in. Lied I suppose and supplied fake papers. He went out on patrol for the first time last week and never came back. He was skinny, so his sargent sent him down a tunnel to find Gooks. An explosion collapsed the tunnel. We hope he was killed by the explosion, but guys seem freaked that he was buried alive. If you ask guys what the worst way to be killed is, they'll tell you they never want to be stuck in one of those damn Gook tunnels.

War isn't good. You wouldn't know that of course because you never went to war. You were in the Coast Guard.

[A voice yells "Coast Guard!"]

There Dad. You see what I mean. Being in the Coast Guard is nothing like being in war.

A pal of mine, Josh Malcolm, the guy who yelled, got himself a friend yesterday. At a party on leave in Phan Rang. He met a local girl who swept him off his feet. And no she's not a hooker, she's an Army nurse. A real American nurse. And no he's not married already, I know what Mom thinks. But she's wrong. Lots of the guys fool around sure, but most of the married guys all stay pretty much loyal. Anyway he showed us a photo of his new girlfriend and she's a real looker.

[Laughter. Cat call whistle.]

Oh yeah, we watched "Casino Royal" last night, the weekly movie in the big tent. I expected a good James Bond film, you know, to get a guy ready to fight again but was a comedy. Funny, sure, but stupid too. Still we do get the occasional new movie. Watched "Cool

Hand Luke" a couple months ago. That was a good movie. That's a movie you'd like Dad.

You remember Dad? When all us kids rode to the drive-in with you and Mom. The three of us in the back seat, popcorn everywhere. And Harry sometimes said the dialog as if he'd seen the movie before but hadn't. Sometimes he made me mad how smart he was. But other times, I miss him.

[Silence with scratch sounds]

I have your letter someplace. Oh yeah. You said, "Tell me if you know anything about that Jo Bailey guy."

Okay, I guess the time's come to tell you about my draft board experience. I hope you don't find that day as weird as I did. I know how much you and Mom hate that guy, that Jo Bailey.

You surprised me when you said Jo Bailey became an item because Sis fell for him at a party. Well that sounds like Sarah, she was always such a damn flirt. I mean she went after the first cute man at any party. And to tell the truth I'm as surprised as you that she decided to move in with Jo Bailey.

You remember her senior prom? I swear, must have been fifteen or twenty guy asked her out. She was the most popular girl in high school, and prom queen too. I remember her mostly as stuck up in high school. I was in Junior College then as you know, and my circle of friends and hers were not ever the same. And she refused to talk to me about her love life. Maybe she talked to Mom, I wouldn't know.

Events of 1966
Neil Allen Fitzpatrick, Ph.D.

"My Years Of Protest" (unpublished) the Chapter titled, "Fun and Games with Jo Bailey." Written while he was still in graduate school at the University of California at Berkeley

A week after the police car speech, we both sat upstairs in Sproul Hall, part of a sit-in. Please remember that sit-ins were new on campuses back then and we really didn't know what to do. I still had my rope because I hadn't strung my clothesline at home yet. I fed out my rope and told everyone to tie themselves together. A good idea at the time, but later an older student with bushy hair came by and made us take that rope off.

"What's going to happen?" Jo asked me.

"Just rumors. Maybe police are going to try to arrest us all."

Jo laughed. "I don't think they have that many police cars."

Someone ran upstairs and yelled. I couldn't understand at first, but then, as he drew closer his voice became clear, "Buses. They brought big prison buses up behind the building! And there's hundreds of cops. I mean hundreds!"

A curly-haired woman shoved an elbow into me as she tried to slide up tighter against the wall. "Excuse me," I told her.

"I don't want to be arrested," she whimpered.

"I'm Raz," I said. "Why have you joined? Why, if you don't want to be arrested?"

"Whinny," she said.

I reached across and shook her hand. "Whinny like the horse." Her hand was really warm.

"No," she said, and yanked her hand from mine. "My boyfriend is somewhere, but I lost him."

From unseen down the hallway a smooth female voice started to sing and pretty soon everyone joined in. I recall, "We shall overcome," or something like that. One of those noble gospels turned civil rights songs. You know the kind.

Downstairs an official voice echoed on a megaphone. Around us the singing quickly faded away. A man's voice boomed, "You are involved with an unlawful assembly. If you do not disperse immediately we will arrest you for criminal trespass. If you resist arrest, you will be charged with that crime too. I repeat, you are on private property and you are all trespassing. Disperse or be arrested!"

Whinny next to me grabbed my arm and held on tightly.

Jo appeared undisturbed. He gazed upward wound up in his own thoughts. At that moment, he seemed a mystic in a trance.

Everyone started to sing again. Christmas songs, the popular kinds like, "Silent Night" and "Jingle Bells."

A man came by to let us all know there would a presentation on the third floor about how to be arrested.

"Will they provide training too?" I asked him.

"Yeah, and there's study space set up too."

Jo and I stood. Whinny remained seated, her arms wrapped around her knees, her head bent down. She struck me as an abandoned sheep among protestors.

"Let's go up to the third floor," I said to Jo. "And learn how to be arrested."

But Jo grabbed my arm. "The Mexican," he said. "I must save the Mexican."

I looked around, "What Mexican?" I asked. Understand we called hispanics Mexicans back then.

Jo looked around too. "I don't see him," he said. "He fell and bounced and fell again. But he looked odd like everything was sideways."

I looked around. "You mean like he fell out a window?"

"Maybe," Jo said. "I'm not sure."

"Let's go up. Maybe he's upstairs."

Third floor wasn't as crowded. We looked for someone presenting a talk but we could only find a music stand set up like a podium but with nobody there. A fellow in a Mexican serape waked back and forth telling everyone to, "Stay out of the offices. Stay out of the offices." I was certain he was stoned on something.

"Is that him?" I asked Jo. "Is that your Mexican?"

"No," he said, in a flat voice.

The first police came upstairs at a little before four in the morning. Nearly everyone was asleep, so their arrival came as a big surprise to us. Governor Brown (the first, not Moonbeam) took that long to okay those arrests. Their noise woke us up on the second floor where we had tried to sleep.

Police marched single file upstairs right past our floor to the third floor. For some strange reason, they decided to arrest everyone up there first. Jo and I stood with a crowd of others and watched the arrests. The police said, "You can walk or be dragged. If you don't want to be arrested, leave immediately."

A few people left. Most wanted to be arrested. A few were dragged limply downstairs, their feet made an awful pounding on those steps. After that, most agreed to walk down.

Police had cleared the third floor and started on our floor. By then the sun had already come up. Body odor was pretty ripe. Jo leaned against a wall with his eyes closed. I nudged him. His eyes snapped open.

I whispered to him, so others nearby wouldn't hear, "I think we should get arrested first, so we can rest."

Jo nodded and muttered, "I hope I can save the Mexican."

"Me too," I said. But I still had no idea what he meant.

Police led us down to the first floor landing where a table was set up. We were searched and they took our fingerprints. They gave us paper towels to wash off ink, but the paper didn't work well. We were marched by other cops down to those buses. I noticed that girl Whinny asleep, her face leaned against a window in the bus behind ours as we walked past.

Events of 1963
Bonnie Wikkens

A letter discovered by her oldest daughter six months
after Bonnie's death of cancer.

I replayed that kiss and sneeze in my mind as I
cut back through the woods. I got back tired and hungry and in time for dinner. My moccasins were wet so I
changed back into tennis shoes with socks.

Esther's and my group were "yellow," and Jo's
group was "green" so we ate at different times. Jo was
in a cabin with two dads and six boys. His "green"
group really meant two cabins full of boys and dads
closest to canoes and furthest from outhouses.

Cabins lacked bathrooms inside them. Instead
we had to use a group of six green painted wooden outhouses located toward the beaver-dam-less creek end
of camp. Adults could come and go whenever they
wanted, to smoke or use outhouses. But only one kid
at a time from each cabin could go to an outhouse. A
kid had take the only flashlight from a hook by the door
and return to the same hook when done. No kids were
allowed outside without a flashlight after dark. Even
older kids like Jo.

After our group of moms and girls had finished
dinner, we passed their group of dads and boys.
Women greeted their husbands with hugs and girls
mixed briefly with boys. Esther quickly found Jo and
whispered something in his ear.

I grabbed her by her elbow and asked, "What did
you tell my foster brother?"

"Don't eat any chili."

"But I already did."

"Then be first in line at the outhouses," she smiled a tight smile at me and drifted away.

I wandered back after that and watched the guys eat. Jo sat next to our foster-dad William. Jo sniffed as if the chili smelled really good. Dinner was the same as we had, chili dogs with big bowls of corn muffins and baskets of apples and pears.

"My stomach doesn't feel good," Jo said to William. "I think I swallowed creek water. Maybe I'll eat an apple."

"That's melted snow," Freddy the instructor said, as he set a ceramic pitcher of water neatly center-table. "Purest water you'll find anywhere. Why you could bottle and sell that water."

Of course I laugh at that. I mean who back then would have thought you could sell bottled water?

William, our foster-dad, felt Jo's head. "You don't feel hot. Why don't you take some fruit and head back to our cabin. I'll bring you some aspirin from our car after dinner."

"I'm okay."

"No you're not," He patted Jo on his back. "Not like you to not eat. You should go back to our cabin and lay down."

I walked back with Jo.

"You're not eating because of that Esther," I told him.

"No," he said. I guess he didn't know I already knew. "I really don't feel good. Something bad will happen. I have to save her."

"What do you mean?"

"I don't know."

"You can tell me. Remember you told me about your mother. You can tell me about anything." I reached to take his hand.

He frowned and crossed his arms. "Not that simple," he said. "I have to save her that's all." He walked past me.

I stood there and watched him walk away and wanted to cry, but I was suddenly hit by a wave of diarrhea. —Just as extreme as I later experienced on that trip with your father to Mexico. I said, "I need to poo." Then I dashed as fast as I could to the closest outhouse. I had the runs, and had them really bad. When I finally stepped out another younger girl pushed in past me.

"I gotta go," she said. "Real bad. Really really bad."

"So do I," a younger boy complained from a line that had formed. "I think I have door-era."

Cabins quickly emptied. Jo, I imagine, was left alone, singularly not sick. Esther's words came back to me, "Don't eat the chili." I have to admit I admired her guts, but still hated that she was after Jo and would go to such extremes to get him.

I looked for Jo and found him as he tiptoed down his cabin front steps and sat down on the bottom step. He kept an eye on the canoes as the day grew darker and darker. Outside, there in the woods, night falls much more quickly then in the city. There are no street lights to keep night and darkness at bay. The sky became black with unbelievable stars.

As darkness fell, several long lines stretched out from each outhouse, boys and girls, men and women, moaned and squirmed. A woman opened the door to one and yelled, "We're out of toilet paper!"

"No we're not!" a lady camp counselor yelled as she raced past me with two large paper bags full. "I have lots more!"

Events of 1970
John Mellion, PFC U.S. Army

Transcript from an audio tape sent to his parents after his death.

Anyway, I drift off topic and have used up a quarter of the tape already. Must be the heat makes my mind wander. My hand sweats as I hold a metal microphone. I swear, everything makes me sweat.

Say that reminds me of a joke. One of the guys said there are actually four seasons in Nam: hot, really hot, too hot, and are you kidding me!"

[Laughs]

Anyway, back to Jo Bailey. At the Oakland Induction Center. The one with all the protesters outside with all their silly protest signs. You know the one's that say we kill babies, and trust me. I've never see a single baby killed. Not one. Not ever. We don't fight like that. If anyone kills babies its the Air Force.

Anyway, me and easily a couple hundred other guys were there because of the draft. Our physical was the last step before I was drafted. Oh, and thank Mom again for turning me into the draft board. I almost got clean away.

[Laughs]

Anyway that's where I met Jo Bailey for the only time.

The place was an old wooden and brick building like in the pictures in Life magazine only in color. Looked like an old high school to me, the kind in the movies, with stairs up the front and lots of windows. Or like in the horror movies where they would split up and get killed in different corridors. You know, with hardwood floors everywhere. Like a basketball court floor but a corridor. All those shoes echoed and all those in line shuffled. Of course I now know that's standard with the Army. The wait I mean. We seem to hurry then wait all the time. Last patrol for example we had to hurry to get ready because the word to deploy was arrived late. Then we were all assembled by the airfield when we found out the choppers had to be refueled first. So we sat there in the sun and waited and waited.

I waited a long time in the induction center too, then my turn came. I was told to undress except for my underpants and was handed a bag to put everything in. I checked my bags at the counter and got a number with a safety pin attached. Ha! We looked pretty silly; all in a line in our underpants. A few guys clipped the numbers on the front of their underpants.

[Laughs]

Then of course, like the actual military, we waited again; along the wall of a big room with high lights suspended down the center of the ceiling. If I hadn't been in the induction center I would have thought maybe I was in a library. You know, with table in the middle and shelves down the side instead of a room filled with guys who hung out and waited. After a while a small bunch of us were moved into another room and told to stand in a line and face forward toward a desk with nobody there.

Jo Bailey stood next to me. A normal enough guy. Thin with brown hair, very middle class.

"I'm John Mellion," I said to him.

"I can't save anyone," he said, but didn't look at me.

"Huh?"

"Oh sorry," he looked at me. "Jo," he said. "Spelled J O. Jo Bailey." He stuck you his hand and we shook. "I'm back for my third time."

"Why. How come you keep coming back?"

"I'm 1Y, you know," he said. "Temporarily incompatible with military service." He pointed to the back of his head and said, "I got a hole up there."

I asked him. "How come your hole can't be fixed?"

He shrugged, then said, "That's not all."

"What do you mean?"

He looked straight ahead when he answered, and I found that kinda creepy. "I can tell when people are going to die, but I can't save them," he said.

The guy on the other side of me said, "Bullshit," and that's how I felt too. Jo, I felt sure, was wacko.

One of the Army doctors started down the line. He looked like all the other actual soldiers but wore a stethoscope around his neck and a white smock over his uniform. He yelled, "Quiet." Then he began at the end of the line. He stopped at each guy, looked him over, asked a few questions, like, "Does that foot hurt?" Then he checked boxes on his clipboard and handed the guy a colored slip of paper. Some got a yellow slip and went to a psych test, others got a blue slip and had to have their blood tested which meant for certain you were about to be drafted. The guy on the far side of Jo went to the psych test. I didn't like the guy's attitude and thought a psych test suited him.

Jo was next. The doctor was close enough so I could tell he was younger than I thought. I guess his long face and pronounced forehead made him look smart. He looked old, but up close his face was young. The doctor looked Jo over with a nod and asked him, "How come you're sweating?"

I looked at Jo and sure enough he was really sweating and his eyes were wide open, I mean really wide like in the movies when someone sees a monster or a ghost. But not scared wide. More I guess surprised or maybe wide because of darkness.

Anyway Jo said to the doctor, "Under a palm tree. You'll die under a palm tree. A single bullet through your helmet." That's what he said. Then he added kinda sadly, "I don't see a baby afterward."

I looked closer at Jo and he didn't look so much frightened as wary. He eyes seemed to gaze at something through and behind the doctor.

But the doctor was unfazed. He pulled out a yellow slip, scribbled something on it and told Jo to go for the psych test. But Jo didn't take the slip. Instead he seemed to stiffen and let out a small sound like a groan or a growl.

I felt his hand grab my wrist. His strength was unbelievable. I mean like a vice or one of those jungle snakes from the movies. Really tight so my hand hurt. I could see the muscles in his arm, they stuck out like they spasmed or something.

The doctor took a step back because Jo began to shake. I wanted to step away too but I couldn't. I used my other hand to try to push Jo's hand off mine but he was so wet with sweat my hand slipped off his. You know, like in a movie when you try to grab a rope but its wet and you slip off and fall back into the river then another snake gets you. Of course the snakes in Nam aren't that big. But there are some poison ones. You have to keep your eyes peeled on patrol and extra peeled when you're under trees. The "two-step" snake that's supposed to be the worst. A little, black, fast one that can kill you before you take two steps. But I don't know anyone that's been bit by one yet. Knock on wood.

[Knock-knock sound]

Well, all of a sudden Jo went quiet and dropped to the floor. He fell straight down like his legs had been pulled out from under him. He yanked me down with him and I fell awkwardly. I must have tried to break my fall because I jammed my thumb and broke a bone. Tell mom that didn't keep me out of the draft though.

[Laughs]

Some real soldier ran over and pulled his hand off mine. Wasn't easy for them either. My left hand was on fire because of my broken thumb. They put us each on a stretcher and told us an ambulance had been called. I lay on that stretcher. Canvas with a wood frame and they left us on that hardwood floor. I wondered, as I lay there, if I would feel so uncomfortable if ever wounded. You know, stuck on a stretcher on the hard dirt. I notice wounded guys and they're either on the dirt or on a cot. The only stretchers I've seen are used to carry wounded to an evac chopper. So I guess you could say the floor in the induction center was like the floor of a chopper, but without flight of course.

[Laughs]

Well a bunch of guys in underpants gathered around to ask questions. I don't remember what they asked because the pain kinda kept my attention more on me. I looked up. Their privates made me uncomfortable. Jo had stopped shaking and he lay there quiet-like. I guess his view up guy's underwear didn't bother him as much as it bothered me. Or at least he didn't say anything. Not that he's a fag, of course, or he wouldn't be with Sarah.

Events of 1966
Neil Allen Fitzpatrick, Ph.D.

"My Years Of Protest" (unpublished) the Chapter titled, "Fun and Games with Jo Bailey." Written while he was still in graduate school at the University of California at Berkeley

I fell asleep on our bus and didn't wake up until we arrived at, what I later found out, was Santa Rita Rehabilitation Center out in Dublin. I didn't really notice our bus until after we arrived. Black bench seats like on a school bus. Our prisoner seats were separated from the driver and a guard by a heavy screen with a door in its center. A cop banged the metal edge of that door with his baton. "Wake up air-heads. Everybody off the bus."

We were marched off, single file, through an open gate and into what looked like an exercise yard. While we waited, a man behind me started to whistle that "Whistle While You Work" song from Disney's "Sleeping Beauty." He whistled until a cop told him to, "Shut up."

Jo stuck by me.

"Nothing to worry about," I told him. "The earliest we can get bail is Monday so we can sleep for two days if we need to."

"I'm not nervous," Jo said. "I'm ready."

We were taken in groups of six out of the yard and down a corridor past some occupied cells. A Mexican guy ran up to the bars on our right and yelled directly at Jo.

"You," he yelled and spit. "You there. God boy. You wanna see something? You wanna see me die?" Those were his exact words, I recall them distinctly.

Jo looked at him, eyes wide. We both had stepped backward away from that crazy Mexican when he rushed the bars. I could see Jo recognized him. I realized he must be the Mexican Jo had told me about. I felt Jo brush past me as he took a hesitant step forward. Just then the two cops who had escorted our group inside rushed past us to deal with the Mexican.

Pale arms snaked out from the cell behind us and grabbed Jo around his throat. Jo looked surprised and confused. A man's face appeared behind Jo, a startlingly pale face, probably albino with pink eyes and a head covered with wildly-white curly hair. "You," he hissed. "You God boy."

Jo tried to say something but his breath had been cut off by those strong, pale arms around his neck. Albino man forced Jo's head sideways in a way that didn't look comfortable. I wanted to help Jo but you have to understand that scene. Too chaotic, with police and real criminals around. And yes, I am ashamed of my inaction.

The Mexican across from us backed quickly away as those two cops rushed forward. "Watch me," he said to Joe. "Watch me die."

The Mexican turned and ran towards the rear wall of his cell. He put his head down and ran full speed away from us. He hit that wall with a horrible loud thump.

The two guards yelled together, "No!". One of them blew a whistle and bellowed, "Bring the key for fifty-two. And get a medic."

Albino man released one arm and used his freed fingers to force Jo's eyes open. "You'll watch God man. You'll watch and see how your God can't help you."

The Mexican stumbled a bit then straightened and squared his shoulders. His face and shirt were soaked in blood. He walked back towards us, toward Jo, his left foot dragged a bit with each step. Blood dripped from his slack finger tips.

45

Other men in the cell with that Mexican hugged the walls to stay clear of him. They all looked as freaked out as I felt.

"You watch me," the Mexican yelled at Jo, his voice slurred. "You watch me die."

Behind me an albino man whispered those same words in unison with the Mexican, "You watch me die."

Another guard ran down the hallway. He opened a gate with a loud clack and came into our hallway. "Keys," shouted to one of the other guards. "Step back, I'll open the gate."

The Mexican turned and ran full speed again, head down, at the far wall. He hit with an even worse thud, and dropped like a stone. As if his soul had been sucked out of him. He fell and didn't move.

The third cop finally got that cell open.

I looked back at Jo. His eyes roll up into his head. I thought he'd been strangled. But he stiffened. That move so surprised albino man that he released Jo.

"You can't stop death," albino man said, as he slipped backward into his cell like a ghost. "You can't stop death."

Jo buckled, then fell and landed fetal-like his side. He began to shake.

"Good god," said one of the protestors. "He's having an epileptic fit."

More cops rushed in. One hefty guard grabbed my arm and led me and another guy out and down another hallway, and left Jo behind. They put us into a cell with a dozen others. One of those was Whinny but she was asleep. I asked the guards but they wouldn't tell me anything about Jo or the Mexican.

Next day we signed agreements to appear in court and were all released on our own recognizance.

I tried to find Jo after that, but he'd already dropped out of school.

I asked around to find out who albino man and the Mexican might be, but they might as well have never existed. I didn't hear anything about Jo until years later when I found Jo's first book for sale at Stacy's bookstore in San Francisco. All I could find in that book was one sentence that reminded me of that day in Santa Rita:

> "That pale man with breath of mint told me
> the truth. I cannot prevent death. I can
> anticipate, I can see death's approach. But
> I cannot prevent death. I can never stop
> the inevitable. That pale man was a
> murderer and a prophet. He taught me an
> important lesson, one deeper and more
> mysterious than he could ever have
> imagined."

Was that, I wondered, Jo Bailey's struggle in life? To try to save the lives of those whose deaths he foresaw? To look at a person and know that person will die and yet to know with equal certainty that nothing can be done to save that person?

Am I Queequeg? Like in Herman Melville, I carve my coffin, unaware that coffin might later become a lifeboat. But a modern Queequeg whose death can be foreseen. If I could have known for certain that I would not have been killed by the whale, would I have lived my life differently, would I have planned for a different future, would I have carved a lifeboat instead of a coffin?

An immortality elixir would be expensive if such an elixir could exist. Just the same, a foreseen certainty of a long life could be worth quite a lot too. Too bad I hadn't thought to ask Jo back then when I briefly knew him. Too bad indeed.

Events of 1963
Bonnie Wikkens

A letter discovered by her oldest daughter six months
after Bonnie's death of cancer.

I sat on our porch and watched as kids, and
adults too, broke one at a time in panic and dashed up
into the trees above camp. I had already relieved myself
so I didn't feel so bad. I was amused to watch.

"Take toilet paper," yelled that same lady camp-
counselor. "And be careful up there. There's poison oak
everywhere!"

When I thought the dark was enough to be safe, I
trotted over and sat down next to Jo. "You seeing that
girl Ester later?"

He looked at me with his eyes downcast. "I need
to save her," he told me. "I need to save her from
water." Then he stood and trotted in the direction of the
canoes.

I waited until he was a goodly distance away,
then I followed him.

He hugged the line of cabins and went the long
way around the picnic tables to avoid being seen. When
he reached the edge near woods beyond the beached
canoes, he stopped and looked around. Dim pine
trunks and black trees towered overhead. I lost sight of
him, he was a dark smudge among darker trunks of
trees.

I was afraid to get too far away from the outhouses but followed him anyway. I wasn't sure what he
meant by, "Save her." I crouched behind the last picnic
table.

"Hi," Esther's voice came from out of sight.

Jo spun in place. Esther appeared and pounced on him. She grabbed him in a firm hug and gave him a long kiss on the lips.

I froze. I didn't want to watch, I didn't want them to see me.

Jo pushed her away and said, "Don't worry, I'll save you."

"Not in the open," Esther said. I don't think she listened to him. "Too much light."

Jo looked around and nodded.

I agreed with Esther. All the cabin doors were open and dumped light and outhouses were ablaze with flashlights that scanned the sky as if for aircraft.

"In the woods," Jo suggested. "That's safe."

"Hmm. No, too spooky."

"In a canoe? I mean on shore?"

Esther laughed and had to cover her mouth to keep herself quiet. "Too hard," she said. But maybe that's me as I look back. You know, with my later experiences under my belt, or maybe you don't know. Well that's enough of that.

Ester looked around. She squinted and looked offshore into darkness. "The swim platform," she said, and pointed. "We can't see it, so nobody else can."

I realized she was right. The swim platform was nearly invisible out in that inky black lake.

Esther took Jo's hand and tried to walk him towards water. "Let's swim," she said.

Jo resisted her pull. "But you can't swim."

"I can swim fine," she said. "I can swim as good as you."

"But I'm not wearing a swim suit. So we can't swim."

"Neither am I silly." Esther bumped him shoulder to shoulder. "Let's swim in our underwear."

Ester shook free Jo's hand and ran to the water's edge. She shed her clothes awkwardly.

Jo trotted up to her and tried to grab her, but she pulled free, waded quickly out and dove. Jo quickly pulled off his shoes, yelled, "I'll save you," and waded in after her.

I had to leave then, because I felt a second terrible poo approach fullness. I dashed back toward the chaos of those long outhouse lines.

I couldn't find Jo after that and didn't see him again until later that night after the police came. I asked Jo what had happened. He told me and —I cried.

Events of 1974
Harry Mellion
Owner of Harry's Home Diner Pismo Beach, California

Please understand. I did not intend to insult my parents when I invited Jo Bailey to Christmas dinner. Jo had been Sarah's (my sister's) husband and, after her death, I felt sorry for him. I knew he lived alone, so I invited him. It took me a while to track him down. Turns out he moved a lot and sometimes didn't leave a forward address. Anyway, I left messages and eventually he called me. I figured he was part of the family, after all, my former bother-in-law, and I thought he could use a little Christmas cheer. I mean, I knew I could use some cheer, so why not?

He seemed surprised that I was still friendly with him.

"What about your Mom and Sarah?" he asked me.

"You didn't kill Sarah. Cancer did."

"But your folks. Won't they be bothered to have me over?"

"Look," I said. "Dinner's at my place. A when they're on my turf they have to be polite, don't they?"

He agreed to come to Christmas dinner at my place and that was that.

You see, that year's Christmas was my turn to host; a family meal at my house, the one I owned back then, in Pismo Beach, my house that overlooked the Pacific Ocean. But Mom telephoned me early that December and insisted we have Christmas at her and Dad's house out in Livermore. I had already invited Jo, of course, but forgot to mention that little fact to Mom. I kicked myself later, of course.

I called Jo back but had to leave a message. I told him to go to my parent's place in Livermore instead of to my place. I told him to call back only if he couldn't meet me there.

He never called back so I presumed all would be okay. You see my sister Sarah moved out when I was away at college. She moved in with Jo and they eloped to marry. For reasons I never understood, Sarah broke off contact with her family, me included. I never knew anything about her, until the day Jo called my parents to tell them that Sarah had died of cancer. My mother blamed Jo. My dad blamed nobody and I blamed the cancer.

Events of 1970
John Mellion, PFC U.S. Army

Transcript from an audio tape sent to his parents after his death.

After a while the guys in underpants were hustled off somewhere else, and Jo and me were taken to county hospital in an ambulance.

The siren and the bumps made for a terribly rough ride. Reminded me of the time a car hit me as I rode my bike home from school. How the ambulance was so warm inside because of winter weather. But in Oakland the inside of the ambulance was cold because of summer heat outside. Of course Nam's hot both inside and out except for the officer's quonset which I was inside of only once and that was air conditioned.

[A yell in the background]

Sorry dad, I have to go. I'll have more to tell you when I get back from patrol.

[a click]

Hi Dad. I'm back from patrol, actually the second patrol, since I last recorded anything. Lots of activity around camp. They shipped platoons up north someplace. We were ordered to tear down our tent and pack up. We sat on our rucksacks in the rain and waited again. There's a joke about rucksacks. No matter how tightly you roll everything, what once fit in your rucksack won't fit again. And nothing does!

[Laughs]

I should turn the recorder off and pack up. I don't want this recorder wrecked in the rain cuz other guys want to send recordings home too.

[a click]

Hi Dad. Still hot as hell but we have some off time. Oh yeah, its two weeks later. Sorry.

You remember Josh Malcolm, the guy that yelled in the background? The guy who had the new girlfriend that was a nurse? Well he died on the first day of patrol. His leg got all shot up and he thought his leg would have to be amputated. But they must have hit an artery because he bled to death before the evac chopper could arrive. I don't know if he left a letter for anyone, he never told me. I do leave a letter, of course, a letter to mom every time we go on patrol. In it, I tell her its her fault.

[Laughs]

Anyway, I got drunk on whiskey last night and I'm a bit hung over. Oops, I forgot Mom would listen to this too. Sorry Mom but you're the reason I'm in Nam.

We're in a new place called Nha Trang. There's a beach called China Beach with snorkel diving. Some of the guy's want to surf but all the surf boards have been claimed by guys that got to the beach ahead of us.

[Laughs louder]

We have to be careful along the beach because the Gooks try to sneak in from the north at night. We don't have to worry from the west though, because the land is flat, filled with claymores and fougas drums. Claymores are like mines but we set them off with wires. And fougas drums are 55 gallon drums of jet fuel that can be set off with a flare. So you see the west is okay and the beach can be okay if you're careful.

But the bugs! The bugs are worse but at least the rain stopped. Or maybe the bugs are worse because the rain stopped. Hard to tell. Mostly its mosquitoes at night like always but add to that the biggest cockroaches you've ever seen. One guy from Texas says they're bigger there but I don't believe him. They hang out on the tent walls. When you squash them ugly green stuff leaks out and stinks. Like I said, the bugs are worse.

Food's better though. The meat has a different label and is not salty like the old stuff. Still brown with brown gravy but tastes better. That and bread and a good cold beer and I'm barely human again.

Tell Mom the food reminds me of her Thanksgiving turkey. That tender, so you can cut it with a fork. And speaking of Thanksgiving I miss you guys. I miss the old home with my own bedroom and our big yard, and no bugs. Yeah, no bugs. Not big ones anyway. And TV every night. Yeah I miss that too.

I hope you hear from Sarah. Not like her to not write. I mean she was always the good kid. You know the sister who would always write home no matter what. The sister that would always send Christmas cards. Like some of the guys here. They made their own cards. They folded and cut paper and colored with ink pens. One of the guys in the other platoon sent fifty Christmas cards. And don't ask, I didn't send any. But then you know that of course. Christmas was last month. The season's don't make much sense where the days are hot all the time.

I'm sitting alone for once in our tent. I sit on my cot. A big tent. There's six cots but only room for four, mine's nearest the door, really a tent flap. The guys have taped up pictures of wives and girl friends above their cots. I don't have any above mine. Just never got around write anything. You know of course that Trina broke up with me after my first letter to her. Said a long distance relationship couldn't work. Hell! I mean what does she think, that war is a five day-a-week commute?

Watched "The Graduate," last night. Talk about a raunchy movie but where the good guy get's the girl in the end. The guys whistled and hooted through the movie so I didn't hear all the words but what I did hear sounded good. If you see that movie Dad, don't take Mom. Might be too strong for her. You remember how she reacted when she found those Playboy magazines under my mattress.

[Brief chuckle]

Anyway, more about that Jo Bailey guy because you asked and there's more to tell.

Like I said last time, we were hauled to county hospital there in Oakland. I got my hand put in a cast and was given some pain pills. Then they made me wait in the hall to fill out some paperwork. The pain pills were really good, I still hurt but didn't seem to mind the hurt. I can see how people can get hooked on that stuff. Not me of course, but if I ever did I'd blame Mom.

[Laughs]

Jo showed up a little later. He stumbled in and recognized me. He dropped into the chair next to mine. Hard wooden chairs lined one wall and all faced a nurse behind a window. Still daytime and sunshine caused the window to glare in my face. Venetian blinds, maybe. The sunshine was behind Jo and made his hair shine like in the movies.

"How do you feel?" I asked him.

"Okay," he said. He didn't sound too sure. His eyes were bloodshot and he looked weak. Afternoon already, but he looked like he had just woken up.

"Did they look at the hole in your head?"

"Yeah," he said, but his voice was kinda flat. "They told me the hole was infected and might infect my brain."

"Jesus!" He sound a little crazy, but I never thought there could be anything that seriously wrong with him. I mean actually wrong. An infected brain. I mean wow. Anyway I asked, "What are they going to do?"

"They said they have to operate. They told me to wait while they got ready for the operation. I guess they thought this was an emergency."

That's all he said, but he acted really worried. Naturally I thought he was worried about the operation.

"Hey," I asked him. "Can you look at me and tell me when I will die?"

He looked me over and apologized. "Sorry," he said. "I can only see death when a few weeks away at most."

"Look hard," I told him. If I'm gonna be drafted, I want to know."

Jo turned to face me on the bench. He stared hard at my face. I could tell he really tried. And in case you wonder, there's nothing special about his stare. If I didn't know better, I'd say he studied my face with freakishly wide open, but bloodshot, eyes.

"Not much," he said, after a while. "Really vague. You die a long time in the future. Under fireworks, maybe. I'm sorry but that's all."

"Thanks." I was relieved then. I'm even more relieved because I checked up on that doctor from the induction center. That is I asked my Lieutenant to check on him for me. Turns out Jo was right. The doctor was shot in the head like Jo said. The first day he was in Nam. Stepped off the plane and wham! Right threw his helmet by a sniper. Blew his brains out through the back of his head.

So fireworks is a good thing, right? That must mean I'll be an old guy and back home. We watch fireworks for the forth of July. And maybe both of you will be there too. Wouldn't that be great? The whole family together again for a forth of July celebration? You know what I really miss, that we can't get here? Watermelon. Ripe juicy watermelon. That's right. And barbecued steak. Man what I wouldn't give for a slice of watermelon and a hunk of barbecued steak. Oh God how I'd love that!

Anyway, back to Jo. He leaned close and whispered to me. "The doctors think I see things that aren't there, because of the hole in my head. I'm afraid that if they fix my head I won't be able to foresee death anymore."

"Would that be so bad?" I asked him.

"Would you like to have your eyes cut out? Would you like to lose you ability to taste food? That's what I'm afraid of. I fear loss of a way to see."

I have to admit I felt sorry for him then. He was a weird guy, sure. But even if he was a fake, the thought he might lose his powers would be bad. I mean like Superman on TV. What if he believed an operation might cure his super powers? Like suppose he had a cavity in his tooth and he was super because of that cavity. Then a dentist fills that hole and wham he's not super anymore.

Well a nurse came by and collected my paperwork. She told me I was done and told me to head back to the induction center. I asked her how and she told me to walk four blocks. She pointed at the window and said, "That way. You can't get lost. Look for all the protesters outside."

I stood, I watched Jo sit with his arms behind his head, leaned back against the wall. He appeared to be lost in thought. I couldn't see anything odd with his head, a mop of normal brown hair. No hole that I could see anywhere.

I said, "Good-bye," to Jo and he nodded. That was that. The last time I ever laid eyes on him. I walked back to the induction center and then they took me, broken thumb and all, and drafted me into the Army.

Well tell Sarah that Jo may be normal, if he got the operation I mean. But I don't know if he ever did.

Events of 1963
Bonnie Wikkens

A letter discovered by her oldest daughter six months
after Bonnie's death of cancer.

When I finally managed to see Jo again, he sat on
the edge of his bed wrapped in a blanket. Midnight and
everyone was still awake, shouts and sometimes weep-
ing outside. I sat on the bed opposite and faced him.

"Bonnie," he said to me. He still couldn't look at
me. "I had another vision. Just like the one when my
Mom died. But this time I witnessed Esther die. There
was darkness and I sensed Esther. She spun her arms,
and windmilled them. I heard bubbles. Then I didn't
hear bubbles any more. She floated face down in daylight bright water with her eyes open. I thought it might
be the lake but I wasn't certain because daytime was
clear in my vision, but the lake was still dark. I thought
maybe she might drown but I couldn't be certain."

Jo finally looked at me. I could tell he'd been cry-
ing because his brown eyes were bloodshot. "Ester ran
into the lake and dove. I tried to swim after her but I
was weighed down by my clothes. The water was cold,
bitter cold. My body became wrapped in a blanket of
sand paper. The top few inches of water were warm,
but all the water below that was ice cold. I looked
everywhere for Ester but couldn't find her in the darkness."

Jo took my hand and squeezed, His hand felt
really cold.

"I listened for her splashes," he said. "And finally
heard them. She was a little ahead of me. I tried to
swim faster, but the cold sucked away my strength too
fast. My strokes became slower and slower. I swallowed

some water and began to choke. Then my knuckles hit wood and I stopped. Somehow I had gotten to the platform."

Jo let go of my hand and sat up straight. "I hauled myself up onto that platform and stood. I looked back and there was only dark flat water. I tried to spot Esther but she wasn't anywhere. And then I must have passed out from the cold. I couldn't save her. I tried, but I couldn't."

Just then our foster-dad William came in and dragged me away. "I don't want you talking to Jo anymore." he said. "Not after what he's done."

I tried to wave good-bye to Jo but he looked at his hands not at me. William dragged me uphill to the parking lot where the other kids waited.

I had my first thoughts about death then, on that dark uphill walk with William's hand holding mine. I wondered if Jo's ability to forsee death meant in some perverse way that Jo could never prevent a death he had foreseen.

Events of 1970
John Mellion, PFC U.S. Army

Transcript from an audio tape sent to his parents after his death.

Well dad, I see the tape is near used up. I'll have to scare up another tape from one of the other guys and I'll have more to say tomorrow.

We're in camp for a few days of R and R. We expect the Gooks to lay off for a few days because the whole country will celebrate a holiday called Tet starts tomorrow. Nice to rest for a while. I wonder if I can get someone to teach me how to surf.

[Laughs]

[the tape ends]

A Letter Accompanied The Tape

Sarah, my dear daughter,

I don't know if I will succeed. You have not answered any of my earlier letters. I imagine you and that Jo Bailey are on a commune together somewhere, maybe in Oregon, or in a Cult. But I took a chance because your mother insisted. To be safe, I put "Please Forward" on the outside.

Enclosed is the last tape your brother ever sent us. Because he talks about you in a way, we thought you should have a copy. I told you in our last letter to you that your brother died in Viet Nam. But in case you threw that letter away unopened, I'll repeat the bad news again.

You must have heard about the Tet Offensive on the news. His commander told us in a letter that John fought bravely. But you and I both know he was never a brave boy. I'm sure he fought out of fear.

If you watched the news then, you'd know that the Tet Offensive looked like fireworks the first night. Deadly fireworks.

Your mother and I have begun to believe what you told us so often when you were still home. That the war is wrong. And yes, you can tell us, you told us so. You mother still feels heavy guilt for turning John into the draft. I forgive her. I hope you can too. Remember what I always say, let bad news roll off your back like water off a duck's back.

Your younger brother Harry is in college at Stanford. Your mother and I pray every night that he never goes into the military. If he did, that would kill your mother. Anyway, Harry says hi. He asked about you at Christmas and we were ashamed we didn't know what to tell him.

Write soon, or telephone, or anything that you can do to let us know you're okay and alive.

Our Prayers Go With You,

With all my love, Dad.

Events of 1974
Harry Mellion

Owner of Harry's Home Diner Pismo Beach, California

Christmas arrived as always, earlier than expected but later than desired. I pulled my car into my parent's two-car wide driveway and parked in front of the closed garage door. When I turned the engine off I realized I'd listened to news instead of Christmas music. I sat there for a moment and remembered Sarah's funeral. My Mom was so furious with Jo she refused to attend the funeral. My Dad said he wouldn't go because Mom wouldn't go. So I took a day off school and went to the funeral but arrived a day late. Her coffin was already at the cemetery poised to be lowered into the ground.

That was were I first met Jo. He looked heart broken and knelt at the foot of her coffin and wept. I walked up and stared at my sister's coffin. I wondered if she was actually inside. But reason told me she was, so I placed my hand on the coffin and felt sadness poke unwelcome fingers hard into my stomach.

Jo noticed me and stood so I introduced myself as her brother and he looked directly at me and said, "I lied to her. I couldn't tell her she would die."

I knew nothing about his abilities at that time, so I became testy. I mean my sister lie in a closed coffin, waited to be lowered into her grave and her husband said stupid things. I said, what I felt was the obvious, "Wasn't that the doctor's job?"

He took a step back as if I had slapped him. And that was when I noticed we were the only two people there. I looked around. The was no sign of anyone in cars either. I asked him, "Are we the only two who showed up?"

Jo looked at me like I was crazy. He asked, "Where's the rest of her family?"

"Her other brother was killed in Viet Nam." I realized I had said, "Her," and that hadn't felt right. But I didn't know what else to say. "Her," sounded like she was still alive. But I couldn't think of a past tense version of "Her."

"I know your brother died," he looked at the coffin. "That audio tape waited for us when we got back from the hospital. The same day we first learned she had cancer."

"God," I said. "Don't ever tell my dad that."

"Look," he said, and walked over to stand by another gravestone next to my sisters. "Your brother is buried there."

That surprised me. I looked around at the cemetery. That's right, the day had been overcast and cold. Just me and my parents and John's friends. "You and Sarah weren't present that day."

"No," he said, and shook his head sadly. "We didn't know he was dead until after he was buried."

"My folks wanted him buried by her. Not in some military cemetery."

Jo looked back at Sarah's coffin so I looked too. Plain white with gold colored trim. More expensive than the one John had been buried in. Jo said, "I miss her terribly."

"Me too." I patted him on the back. "Me too."

That seemed to break the ice between us.

I opened the car door on Christmas day, but continued to sit and wonder. When had Jo and I become more than an ex and brother-in-law? When had I decided I knew him well enough to invite him to Christmas dinner? Not at the funeral. Maybe at one of a handful of dinners at my house. Or maybe the one an only time we had bowled.

"Oh, well," I said aloud. I crawled from the car and walked to my parent's front door. I was the last child that remained. I was the youngest and only one left. I felt like I walked on thin ice even though the day was up in the low 70s, shirt-sleeve weather.

Dad met me at their door and gave me a long hug, a really long hug. I still had not gotten used to his newly developed warm excesses. Dad wore his traditional Christmas sweater, the one Mom had bought him when they were first married. Green with white reindeer front and back. His hug felt fit and strong, his full head of grey hair tickled my nose. He no longer smelled like tobacco and that made me smile.

"Hi Dad," I said, once freed from his hug. "Merry Christmas."

"Merry Christmas son."

"You quit smoking?"

"In June," he smiled genuinely happy. "Six months."

Christmas music played softly on the stereo. One of those crooners, Bing Crosby or Perry Como sang "Silent Night." Just the very music my Mom always liked. The house smelled of roast turkey and pine from a real tree in the living room. "Smells good," I said. "By the way, Jo called and he should arrive around four."

Dad looked at me a little sideways; like he always did when he believed one of us kids lied. "You didn't tell us Jo was coming."

"Sorry," I smiled, then tried to put him at ease. "Christmas was supposed to be at my place and I invited him. You know, as family or ex-family. I guess I forgot to mention that, when Mom switched Christmas back to her house."

Dad was one of those men who had always rolled with the punches. Even when Sarah died, Dad appeared to take the news in stride and instead comforted Mom. I don't think he ever took the time to mourn her death for himself. Everything with him was done for Mom.

"Honey," Dad called to Mom.

"Is that Harry?" Mom asked. She was the sort who would never emerge from the kitchen until Christmas dinner was served. "Send me my boy. I need to flour him up with a big Christmas hug."

Dad shrugged then and smiled at me. He led the way to the kitchen, as if I had never been there before. He was like that, you see, sometimes too oblivious to the obvious.

"Harry's invited a friend," Dad called to Mom as we walked toward the kitchen.

"A new girl friend?" She was always hopeful like that after my divorce.

We entered Mom's world. A recently remodeled kitchen with an island down the center. The oven door was open and a turkey, brown and aromatic, lay part way out on a rack. Mom had just floured and rolled a top piece for the berry pie, our traditional desert. Tin foil covered ceramic bowls of mashed sweet potatoes and cole slaw. Mom wore her traditional green, flour dusted apron covered with holly leaves and berries.

I gave Mom a big hug, and she gave me back an even bigger one, longer. "My dear sweet boy," she mumbled several times while she hugged me.

"Harry invited Jo," Dad said, to break the spell.

I admit I was surprised when mom released me and stepped back. "Jo Bailey?" she asked. Her expression had gone from a smile to a neutral but tense look.

"Yes," I said, but I began to think I shouldn't have.

"Well," Mom said, after a tick or two of the wall clock. "That might be okay. I guess you could kinda think of him as family." But she still didn't smile.

"I'll set another place," Dad offered. "Give me a hand." He pulled me by the arm.

"Merry Christmas," I said to Mom.

"Ok," was all she answered. She covered the pie with the just-rolled sheet of dough. She still didn't smile.

The dining room and living room were two ends of one large area. The dining room was closest to the kitchen and the living room toward the front of the house. The TV was turned on in the living room and a local station broadcast an image of a Yule log that continually burned in a fireplace. A medium sized Christmas tree stood in the corner, no presents underneath, but was covered with all our traditional ornaments from when we were kids.

"I think your Mom still blames Jo," Dad said.

Dad opened the cupboard and took out a set of dishes. "Grab some silver from the drawer," he told me.

I noticed Mom had laid out the fancy Christmas table treatment. A green tablecloth with tassels all around the edge. Then a bright red runner down the center flecked with golden, smiling suns. Matching candle holders set symmetrically offset from center, with multi-colored ornaments in them instead of candles.

Dad set fresh plates on the un-set side of the table, the place where Sarah would have sat. The last time Mom used that setting was when John was in Vietnam and Sarah hadn't left home yet. Since then, since John had been killed and Sarah died of cancer, Mom had only used the everyday white tablecloth for Christmas since then.

I handed the silver across the table to Dad. "Sorry about inviting Jo," I tried to sound sincere.

"What's done can't be undone."

I looked around the big room. "Where are all the photographs of us kids?" There used to be framed photos of us on the mantel and in all the nick-knack shelves and on the TV. In their place were ceramic figurines, geese and winged horses and porpoises.

Dad put his hand on my shoulder and gently squeezed. "Sometimes reminders can be too much," he said, and nodded at the kitchen.

The doorbell rang.

"I'll go," I said, and I started for the door.

"Hold on," Dad said, and stopped me with his hand. "This is still my house. I'll get the door, you go help your mom."

I smiled at Dad. I couldn't help myself, I enjoyed his efforts to hold onto his traditional family role.

In the kitchen I watched Mom carve the turkey. Mom was the sort who liked to carve the turkey in the kitchen and serve slices on a platter. In the other room Dad greeted Jo.

A slice slid off her fork and landed on the counter-top instead of on the serving tray. Mom said, "Shit."

You have to understand that my mother would never, not ever swear. If her mouth was a faucet, the water would rival the purest bottled water from France. I looked at her and noticed her mouth was set. She rescued the dropped slice from the counter with the fork.

"You can carry that and the spuds out," she said. But I could tell she tried to listen to the muffled conversation from the dining room.

I carried the tray and the bowl of mashed sweet potatoes out. Jo was there. He chatted with Dad. Jo spotted me. He leaned across the table and took the tray from me. He set the tray centered on the table and I set the bowl down off to one side.

Jo crossed his arms, stood up straight and looked at me. I felt as if he appraised me. He was nicely dressed in a sport coat and slacks, but no tie. I noticed the sport coat had patches on the elbows. The coat reminded me of a writer's sport coat. "You look more and more like your dad every time I see you," he said.

Dad said, "I'll take that as a compliment." Then he smiled.

Mom appeared at the doorway. She carried a bowl of stuffing and a boat of gravy. She paused in the doorway, glanced at Jo, then looked away and moved in and set her things on the table. She had removed her apron to reveal her special Christmas dress. She set the gravy down with a noticeable thunk.

"Good to finally meet you," Jo said.

"Yes, hi," Mom said. she wiped her hands on her apron and said to Dad and myself, "Let's sit." She sat to my right, directly across from Jo.

Dad hurried around behind Mom and helped her with her chair. "There you go honey," he said, and kissed her from behind on the cheek.

I sat in my usual place at the foot of the table. Jo sat to my left. I noticed he hadn't taken his sport coat off. "The food looks great as always," I said to Mom. I hoped to break the ice.

Dad sat at the head of the table and said, "Yes honey, looks de-luscious."

Mom folder her hands in her lap and cleared her throat. Then she said, "Let's give thanks to God."

Dad folded his hands on the table and hung his head and I did the same.

Jo said, "I don't believe in your God. But I respect your desire to pray."

I looked up with my eyes and I could see Mom stiffen. "Frank," she said to Dad using his first name, "Please."

Dad didn't miss a beat. He thanked God for the food, and for a fine wife, and for leaving him with a fine son.

I said, "Amen," in cadence with my Dad and mom so we couldn't tell if Jo had said amen too.

Mom smiled a brave smile and picked up her fork but she didn't look up. "Let's eat before the food get's cold."

"So tell us Jo," Dad said. "What you been up to these last couple years."

Mom ate with her eyes down, but I could tell she listened keenly. She cut tiny pieces and moved the food from the plate to her mouth quietly with deliberate motions.

"Not much. I got work as a carpenter for a while but never enough hours to get into the union. I've started to consult for money instead of work for free. I've saved up a enough and want to travel. France looks nice." He cut his turkey meat with a knife. He didn't need a knife, of course, because Mom's turkey was so tender you could cut it with a fork.

"Why France?" Dad asked.

"Sarah always wanted to go to France."

Mom dropped her fork on the plate. I looked at her but her eyes remained downcast. She picked up the fork and speared another small piece of turkey. But she stopped there, with the turkey half way between the plate and her mouth.

Jo continued, "Toward the end she studied French and insisted I tried to learn the language too. I don't have a knack for languages though. Not like Sarah did."

Dad leaned toward Jo and said, in a low voice. "Jo. Talking about Sarah might not be good conversation for a Christmas dinner."

"Sorry," Jo said.

We all ate in silence for a while. I took a second helping of turkey and mashed sweet potatoes and poured more gravy over both. I noticed Mom smile when Dad took more too.

"I started writing a book," Jo said, at last.

"What about?" I asked him.

"How I see religion. You know. From my experiences. How memories live on after death. The way faces change to me when a person is about to die. The provable fact that there is no God."

I glanced at Mom. She stared at Jo. Her mouth was set, a piece of cole slaw stuck to the corner of her mouth like she'd started chew when her attention had been drawn to Jo.

"When Sarah caught the flu during her cancer treatments," Jo said. "I walked into the room and sensed that she was about to die. She looked at me and noticed something in my expression. 'Am I going to die?' she asked me. No, I told her. I lied to her to keep her happy. But I betrayed her in a way that was unforgivable. You see, she knew I lied but she smiled at me anyway because she knew I didn't want to hurt her."

We had all stopped eating and listened to Jo.

"After she died I found the memories of a dead woman who was neighbor to her new mother. Memories, you see, to the dead, are like they are still alive. Anyway, I stood in my doorway, the dead woman's doorway, and waited. The mother carried her small baby down the steps and paused next to me. A pretty baby, I said. 'That's so nice of you to say,' the mother said. What's her name, I asked."

"Stop," my mom said, softly. "Stop. Stop."

"Her name—," Jo said.

"No," Mom said, more loudly. She pushed her chair back and stood. The chair made a rubber-on-wood squeal as she pushed back. She put her hands on her hips, then changed her mind and pointed at Jo. "No. My daughter is in Heaven with the Angels. Jesus has taken her in his arms. Jesus has taken Sarah thorough the blessed doorway into heaven."

Because Dad raised me as a gentleman, I stood when Mom stood. Then Dad stood and set his napkin on the table. Jo stood last.

Mom came around the table behind Dad, at Jo. I don't think I've ever before seen such a look of hatred on Mom's face before.

"My daughter was a good girl. She earned her way into Heaven. She's not anybody else's daughter. I don't care what you say, she's up in Heaven."

Mom surprised me. She pushed Jo in his chest and forced him to take a step back. "If that's the way you feel," she said, even more loudly, with a punch to the words "way" and "feel." She pushed him harder. "If that's what you believe, then get out. Get out!"

Dad hurried up behind Mom to try to calm her.

"Get out of my house," she pushed Jo again. "Get out. Get out. If that's what you believe, get out." Each time she pushed Jo further from the table and closer to the front door.

And then Mom seemed to deflate. Her arms dropped.

Dad tried to put his arms around her, but she shrugged him off. She ran up stairs, wailed loudly and slammed the bedroom door hard and left an uncomfortable silence behind.

I turned to apologize to Jo, but found the front door wide open and Jo was gone.

Events of 1963
Bonnie Wikkens

A letter discovered by her oldest daughter six months
after Bonnie's death of cancer.

Years later when I learned physics I learned
about Schroedinger's cat. I'm certain you girls learned
too. A cat in a box is both dead and alive at the same
time, but once that box is opened and we can see that
the cat is either dead or alive, and remains that way
from then on. So I thought the same thing might happen with Jo. Maybe he's the man who looks at all cats
all the time. Once he sees a dead cat in the box, for Jo
that box has been opened and he can never close that
box again, even though he opened the box in the
future.

Thank God we cannot open those boxes. You
remember Penny, how I found her in the bathroom
with her wrists cut. I called 911 and hugged her and
told her how much I loved her. I opened that bathroom
door when I did and found her still alive. But I could
have as easily opened that door maybe an hour later
and found her dead. So I sometimes ask myself, what I
would I do if I knew that she would be dead, no matter
what I did, no matter when I opened the door. How
could I live with such knowledge?

So there's a lesson my darling daughters. If you
ever see a friend act suicidal, your responsibility is to
do whatever you can to make sure you never open any
door too late. Tell their parents, their teacher, the
police, anyone with the authority to protect them.

Sorry Penny.

Well that was the last time I ever knew Jo, before
he was famous I mean and I read his books. Susan,

our foster-mom, hustled all us kids except Jo into the car and we drove off without him. A weird ride home in the middle of the night. All the kids wanted to know where Jo was. Susan told them, "He did something bad." Just that. But I knew better. I knew he had tried to save her. I wanted to tell them I was glad Esther was dead. But I couldn't. His secret was my secret.

Later, maybe a few years later, Jo sent me a letter that I've kept with me always. I have a confession to make. Sometimes, when I'm alone I imagine I have his letter, like before in a box in my closet, I imagine he signed it, "Love, Jo." But he didn't sign it that way. Did he?

Letter from Jo Bailey

Foster Sister Bonnie,

I don't remember much of that last night with you.

I lay face up in a canoe. Water lapped at its sides, and a flashlight shined in my eyes.

Then I was half awake in a bed in one of the "green" cabins. Adults I didn't know yelled hateful things at me. I tried to turn my head away, but William, our foster-dad, sat next to me. You remember how strong he was and how bad he smelled on hot days. He turned my head forcefully to face them. "You'll listen to them," he barked at me mean-like. His eyes were wet like he had cried. I must have passed out again.

I awoke next as many cars started and the sound as they drove off, you probably among them. I was alone in the cabin, wrapped in a scratchy gray blanket. I walked to the front door and looked out. The sun was setting again and the camp was deserted. A police car was parked by the canoes. No lights flashed.

I felt an odd caress across the back of my neck, soft like a cool breeze or the light touch of an ice cold hand. I turned my head to avoid the feeling and stared at the woods far away beyond the canoes. My eyes were drawn to that same place where earlier I had met Esther. I smelled strawberries, distinctly. Esther stood in the distance inside the forest's shadow. She glowed oddly, not brightly with light, but more like a glow that smudged her a little, and made her hard to see. She said something to me that I couldn't understand, I could barely see her lips move, she was too far away. Then her strawberry scent tickled my nose. I sneezed and she was gone.

A policeman and one of the instructors walked toward me uphill toward the door where I stood. The same instructor who taught me how to handle a canoe, the same man who told me creek water was pure, the one with the handle-bar moustache. I knew for certain then that my life was about to take another bad turn. I hung my head and muttered to myself so they couldn't hear me, 'Thanks Esther. Thanks for sticking around.'

And thank you, Bonnie. Even though you were a foster-sister, you were always the best sister a guy could ever have. And you are the only other person in the world, who knows what I mean when I say I am haunted by a ghost.

Jo

Events of 1974
Harry Mellion

Owner of Harry's Home Diner Pismo Beach, California

After Jo walked out, my head seemed to empty itself of all thoughts. I stood there unsure of what had happened.

Dad put his hand on my shoulder. "Son," he said. "Best, I think, you should warn us about friends you might bring to dinner."

"Especially," I agreed. "If that friend is Jo."

He laughed, his good humored laugh. "Looks like we have to wash dishes tonight," he said.

"Yeah," I said. But my mind was still on Mom.

Dad must have noticed the look on my face. He put his hand on my shoulder. "Roll with the punches," he told me. "To survive so much pain you have to learn to roll with the punches."

I wanted to punch him, to yell at him that grieving was okay. But I didn't. I stood there and looked at Dad and he looked at me. After a while he said, "I better go upstairs, you know to. . . ."

I gave him a hug and said, "I know. You go to Mom and I handle the dishes."

"Thanks son," he said, and turned and walked up stairs. He disappeared around the corner and was gone. I cleaned up the dishes and loaded them into the dishwasher. I also put the Christmas table decorations away. I figured Mom would appreciate that. I noticed the lights were off upstairs when I finished so I left and drove home.

A month later to the day, on January 24th, Mom called and told me Dad had passed away. Heart failure she said, from all those years he had smoked.

"Thanks son," those had been his last words to me. "Thanks son."

I ask Mom, "Will you be okay?"

"I don't know," she said. "Without your father to lean on. I don't know."

I wanted to ask her if she wondered like I did why Jo hadn't foreseen Dad's death. But I couldn't ask her. I was certain that I could never, ever ask her anything about Jo.

I tried to picture that Christmas night, but I couldn't. Details had faded. I can't remember if Jo treated my Dad any differently. You know, differently as if he had known. But I couldn't tell. And I couldn't ask Mom.

"I'll come over tonight," I told her.

"Thanks son," she said. But her voice sounded uncertain.

"I'll be there," I said.

"Yes. Thanks," she said, and hung up.

I hung up and looked at the clock. I thought I should wait a bit to avoid the evening commute. I fixed myself a cup of strong coffee and waited. Waited that night to drive to Livermore to be with Mom. Waited that night and wondered about Jo and if he knew about Dad and why he hadn't said anything.

"God!" I shouted. "God how I miss my Dad!"

Part 2

The Middle Years

Events of 1975
Paul Langdon
Adapted from his essays "Paris Waits."

During my first trip in 1970 I met and became friendly with several Yanks. In April I attended a concert of the Doors in the Boston Arena. The place was packed and hot from bodies and filled with smoke. The Doors are a terrific group. I still listen with rapt joy to "People are Strange" and "Light my Fire." In fact the latter plays as I write this essay.

Foolish greetings can be quite common even in myself. For example, a friend of mine is a cinematographer and a dedicated film buff. He loves to drink socially and has too often told me the story of the time he met Richard Attenborough the film director. My friend stood in a reception line and slowly approached his turn to meet the famous director. He had rehearsed several brilliant quips he could use to impress Mr. Attenborough. But when his turn arrived, he blurted out a feeble "Gosh, Mr. Attenborough. I really like your films." My friend always told his story with great amused embarrassment.

After the Doors concert a similar faux pax happened to me. I met a guy named Kevin who "clicked" on my English accent. He held a back stage pass and escorted me to meet the band. That's when I too waited in line and thought up dozens of clever greetings. When I finally met Jim Morrison, I gave him a feeble and embarrassed "Honored to meet you." That is, before I became so much more embarrassed, when I allowed myself to be pushed aside by an army of young women who all pawed him.

Kevin allowed me to "flop" at his place in Brooklyn on the top floor of a "brownstone walk up." — Creaky wooden steps, all the way up four dim flights to the top landing. I won't describe the smell, but I started to vomit but didn't. The walk up those stairs, I must confess, was not easy to do when drunk and a little stoned.

We flopped on an old Persian rug spread on the hardwood floor of an otherwise bare apartment and listened to LPs and talked for hours, mostly about him and how he grew up around rock bands. He told me he was homo, and I told him I wasn't. There was an embarrassed silence, and then we began to talk again. He'd traveled to Monterey Pop on the west coast then two years after that to Woodstock on the east coast.

"Monterey Pop," he told me. "Felt like a new beginning. Everyone shared a common excitement and the bands played as if each and every one lived to play. But Woodstock was different. Woodstock felt like the start of commercialization. The first time I could smell the money surrounding a concert." He knew all the musicians of course, what they played, how each got into the business, and what their strengths and weaknesses were.

Kevin had whetted my taste for all things rock music. I never heard from Kevin again after that brief weekend. I recently got word that he died of AIDs in the mid 80's. Too bad. I mean really, too bad.

Events of 1977
Joanne Tracy

Book Editor (retired) New York, New York, From a
series of taped interviews.

Everyone at Truehouse Publishing knew I was a widow. My husband, you see, was a sous-chef a Bruno's downtown. That is, until drunk he powered his Mustang head-on into the divider of the Sumner Tunnel up near Boston. So I decided to take Jo Bailey for dinner at Bruno's, where I still remained well known, to discuss his manuscript.

He arrived well dressed in a conservative suit and pale tie, but moved as if he were not comfortable in a suit. He frowned a few times while he read the menu then looked up at me. His eyes were a deep brown and his full head of neatly combed hair made him seem handsome, perhaps famous.

"Let's start with drinks," I suggested as the waiter walked up. "A martini with two olives," I told the waiter.

Jo looked up at the waiter and hesitated. "Do you have beer in bottles?"

The waiter listed a dozen brands and Jo selected Becks, the last one listed.

I arched my fingers and looked at Jo. "I was surprised and delighted, when my boss gave me your book to edit. I'm an atheist you see, so I thought I could be professionally objective."

That seemed to surprise Jo. He sat up straight and said, "A philosophy book more than a religious book."

"I read your book, which I appreciated as a work of, well, conviction. Perhaps a somewhat twisted conviction, tempered by its strange resemblance to cult books that are so common these days. But that aside, your book is riddled with syntactic and lexical mistakes that need to be fixed before I can authorize your $1,000 advance." I slid the marked up manuscript across the table to him. "Fix where I have indicated and then we can publish."

He pulled the manuscript close but didn't peek to see what I had marked up. Instead he simply said, "I'll fix everything that needs fixing. You can count on me."

Our drinks arrived and I soon asked lots of questions about him and his past. But he answered my questions with questions of his own. As if he was wary or wanted to remain private. So the conversation drifted to movies and books.

After that meal, he spent six months in Europe. I was surprised after his return to learn he had taken my markups and used them to produce a completely rewritten book, one that ended up twice as long as the first draft.

On the telephone, Jo explained. "Since then I have found I can visit the next life, the life that follows but is somewhere else. I haven't figured out where the next life is yet. One guy I met in Paris suggested in another dimension. An old religious man described another level of existence. But because I can't tell where the next-life is yet doesn't mean I won't solve the problem some day. The next level of existence, that's what I omitted from the book."

"That's fine," I told him. Of course I didn't understand at all. In all honesty I thought he acted spoiled because he was famous. Still, I told him seriously, "You must not keep revising the book every time you get a new idea. We have to fix what we have in hand, and get that to the printer."

"Are you sure? I keep discovering new ideas all the time."

"Yes. If you have more to say, do so in the next book."

There was silence on the line, then he said, "A second book. I hadn't thought of that."

After three months of back and forth we finally had a manuscript that was publishable. The title was originally supposed to be, "The Book of Jo." But Jo, at the last minute, changed the title to, "The 1st Book of Jo," I presume he expected to write and have us publish a second book, but more about that second book later.

Events Of 1978
Barry Goodman

On Death Row, San Quentin, California, Assembled
from a series of interviews performed, in the presence
of his lawyer

Yeah, I was Jo Bailey's bodyguard for a while. I'm
not sure how you found that out, cuz I never told anyone. But you found me and asked the right questions,
so well I guess I should finally spill the beans, or what
beans there are to spill. [laughs] Mostly we eat white
beans most days. but that really ain't as bad as you
think. White beans don't cause the same farts as other
beans. [laughs again]

But so as I don't confuse things, I'll start at the
beginning or at the beginning so far as I relate to Jo
Bailey. Back then, you see, I was driver mostly, not a
body guard, I'm sure you understand the distinction. I
worked for a rich Cuban —and no I ain't gonna tell you
his name. Anyway, a Cuban got himself snuffed in a
bad way, so I needed a new job.

Nothing seemed to come up right away and I
started to think about maybe a move to the other coast,
maybe New Jersey. Then a guy, who knew a guy, gave
me an address to go to up in San Francisco, so I went.

So Jo Bailey lived in a middle sized, two-story
house behind a gate. A taxi dropped me off outside his
gated driveway. Jo Bailey check me out with binocs
from his upstairs window, you know a dormer window
with a flower box and curtains inside. I didn't think
that was wise because the window didn't look bullet
proof and I remembered how the Cuban got killed [law-
yer touches his arm]. Anyway I waited. Too sunny and
hot that day so I sweated inside my suit but I waited

anyway. Finally he buzzed me in. When I got close to the front door he told me he had a gun and to stop. So I stopped.

The house looked modest, not a mansion like I expected, a big house with a big front door and lots of windows. The front door was a step up, I noticed, in addition to the front step. I thought that single step was good because extra steps slow down anyone who tried to rush in.

I explained who I was and that I needed a job. He had me list my background and give the name of the guy whose guy my guy knew. I did all that and he finally let me in the front door and into the air-conditioned interior. I took off my sun glasses as I stepped inside and he noticed me do that.

"What do I call you?" he asked.

"Barry," I sez. "Just Barry."

"Okay just Barry," he said. "You'll drive me everywhere. The car is in the garage, the sedan, not the convertible, and the key on the hook by the front door. The car has bullet-proof windows. You'll walk me in and out of everywhere and jump between me and trouble without a second's hesitation. You up for that?"

"That's what I do."

"You'll live in. I have a guest house out back. That's were you'll stay. When can you move in?"

"That window where you first watched me doesn't look bullet proof," I told him.

Without hesitation, he said, "That window is. All the windows are. When can you start?"

I told him I had to get my stuff shipped up from L.A. but could start anytime. Simple as that. He paid me more than I'd ever been paid before and gave me most weekends off. A pretty cushy job if I don't say so. I moved my stuff in and started the next Monday night. My first job was to drive him to a dinner meeting with some Japanese fellows. The dinner turned out to be no risk at all. That meeting and most after that became really routine. I was always aware of my job of course. But no threats seemed to ever appear.

Mostly the job was pretty usual. Nothing exciting. No great risks or saves. Just drive and watch his back. But that takes me to your first question.

Events Of 1986
Wayne Manley

Sheriff Officer (retired), Needles, California, His story
as recorded on the last three days of his life

My cousin Lester Manley moved back and first joined me and my dad for dinner at my dad's place. Ribs and spuds, I recall, barbecued out back to spare my dad's modest air conditioner from the strain of inside cooking. I was surprised to hear that Lester was prepared to take the Clinic over right after his dad's, my uncle's death.

"What happened to your dad?" I asked him, miffed that my own dad had not told me his brother had died. We all wore bibs because my dad's barbecue sauce was powerful-hot and messy.

"He died last year," Lester said. He was dressed casual like I was, but his shirts were always striped, mine were always plain blue. "After he died," Lester continued. "Well I guess the town was one too many doctors short, so your dad asked me to move back. An easy choice because I inherited my dad's house and clinic."

I realized how much I missed Lester. I'd last known him when dad and my uncle had held their last common Thanksgiving. Lester and I were in high school together then. I was always a year behind Lester because he was smarter than I was. After that Thanksgiving, the stupid feud between my dad and uncle became a wedge between us. Lester left for college and then I did, and we lost track of each other.

He was a man I could call a friend. He was forthright and honest. My dad spoke up before I could, but said what I wanted to say, "So Lester," he smiled which made his wild eyebrows go up. "How bout you join my and your cousin for barbecue every Sunday."

"I'd love to," Lester said. "You mean the feud's over?" Lester laughed, which seemed, to show the question wasn't a serious one.

"Never was a feud," my dad said. But Lester and I both knew there had been one.

I had the idea later to always meet with Lester for breakfast at Juicy's restaurant to kick start each day.

My deputy was ten years older than I was. His name was Andy Wiggs and he turned out to be flaky. I quickly discovered why had never been promoted. He was a sucker for easy women and was often late to work because of that. But despite his late arrivals and despite that he drank sometimes on duty, I liked him and could begrudgingly rely on him.

That was the morning that started everything, the events I mean that caused me to tell my story. A Mrs. Dodson, owner of the Bar-X ranch, who I had heard about, but hadn't met yet, telephoned me that morning. I was on my way out of the office to meet Lester for breakfast when the phone rang. Andy was late as usual so I answered the phone myself.

Her voice sounded crisp and young, but her fussy manner suggested to me she might be older.

"I got a fax yesterday," she said.

"I'm Sheriff Manley," I told her. "Who are you?"

"Mrs. Dodson. You must be new!" Then she continued without waiting for me to reply. "Someone unnamed wants to live in the old rock house. That's the one I own out on Cedar Canyon Road in case you don't know."

I knew that rock house because of its reputation. Kids and drifters who occasionally got hurt out there from broken glass and rusty metal that littered the property. "The rock house is not in good enough shape to live in," I said.

"They promised to fix the place up," she said. "Their fax told me they would install a roof. That and replace the windows, and install an outhouse."

"Sounds okay to me," I told her. "That place has become a real dump."

"That's why I called you," she said. "You know I want to tear the place down. But some folks have petitioned to have that house declared historically significant. I figure, rented and fixed up, well that might take some of the pressure off."

"I'll drive out there and check to see who might be there."

"Thank you, Sheriff. Come out and see me sometime." Then she hung up. And yes, that's exactly what she said, like from the movies, "Come out and see me sometime."

I wrote myself a note and went to breakfast. I didn't get a chance to tell Lester about the call because his divorce had become final and, well, we spent the morning talking about his ex-wife and why he divorced her.

I would have gone to check out the rock house the next morning, but that plane crashed in the Granite Mountains, that light plane from Las Vegas, you know the one with that comic on board, Ozzie Gumps I think was his name. And well, I got so wrapped up in the crash, that I clean forgot about her mystery person at the rock house.

About a month later I drove Lester out Cedar Canyon Road so that he could check up on old Mr. Aloshapman. The old guy lived half way between Needles and anywhere else. He had an on-and-off again heart condition that required a monthly visit by his doctor. I gave Lester a ride because his car had boiled over and was in the shop. And beside, the air conditioning in my squad car, actually a truck, was the top of the line.

Events of 1975
Paul Langdon
Adapted from his essays "Paris Waits."

The second part of my story took place five years later in the summer. That summer was my "grand tour" around Europe. I began in Brussels and worked my way south to Rome, mostly by a sequence of trains. A German woman I met in Rome's Termini train station told me in broken English to not miss Pere Lachaise cemetery in Paris. She listed for me a dozen famous people buried there, ticked each off each one with a snap of her red sharpened finger nails. When she mentioned Jim Morrison's grave, I was hooked.

From Italy I headed north again to Paris. Once there I took the Underground, which they call the Metro. The aptly named "Pere Lachaise Station" led to the surface across the street from the Pere Lachaise cemetery.

The cemetery is located at the east end of Paris in what can kindly be called a working class neighborhood. Four-story residences of an under-maintained and patched appearance, all dingy and shuttered. A high, dirty grey wall extended opposite for a long city block. That wall marked the boundary to the cemetery. The main entrance was about half way along that wall set back from the street and through an arched gated opening.

I arrived in mid morning with the sun not all the way up. Still, the temperature was sufficiently not cold so I was dressed in my shirt sleeves and carried my light travel jacket over my arm. I knew enough French to get by, but lack of confidence caused me to pantomime more than speak.

Just inside the main gate a uniformed attendant said something to me I didn't completely understand. I took his words as a greeting, nodded and smiled and walked past him and into the cemetery.

I really didn't appreciate the cemetery's magnificent size until I began to trudge up the long sloped road into its interior. The road appeared to be a half a kilometer long yet appeared to extend less than half way up the full cemetery. Huge, mature old oak and maple trees towered over marble mausoleums and granite grave stones visible in every direction. Everywhere was a tumble of contrasting statuary, some religious, some military, some ancient Greek. I felt cooler inside under the trees, but the air still promised heat later in the day. I breathed in the quiet there among the graves. Some headstones were dark black and polished while others were pure white.

I turned right past a wall in the center of which were two darkly greened bronze statues of nubile women who cavorted around a large headstone. The tableau appeared vaguely classic but I couldn't place the reference. The name etched in the headstone was for the Families Begnu Krenorst, whoever they were. Adjacent to that wall I ascended steps to the next higher level. I tried to make out names as I walked but none of those seemed famous either. Some were old, so old that the name had become obliterated over eons. Others were brand new and still appeared crisply etched or carved.

I followed the main path up a slight rise and then down again and came to a large circular area shaded by oak trees. In the center was a large round patch of fenced lawn encircled by the walkway. Wood benches bordered the walkway's edge and faced inward across the path and towards the lawn. I spotted a young man who held a small map, seated on one of the benches. He seemed lost to me.

"Morning mate," I said to him and smiled. "You a yank?"

He looked up at me and I was struck by the look in his eyes, maybe sad, maybe lost. "Yeah," he said. He remained seated. "I'm Jo, J O, Bailey" he reached out and we shook hands. I recall that he shook hands like a Yank, one smart shake then let go.

"Pleased to meet you Jo Bailey, I'm Paul. Paul Langdon."

"You sound like a Brit."

"You got me pegged. Sired and raised in London." Jo stood up and I was surprised by how much taller he stood than I. He was lanky and handsome in that American way, like a cowboy from the movies.

Jo smiled and said, "I thought I studied enough French to get by, but I didn't learn nearly enough."

"My predicament is different. I never bothered to learn much French. But I don't care, I love Italian, and isn't that actually the true language of arts?"

"I wouldn't know," Jo said. He folded the map which he tucked into his back pocket. "I don't pay any attention to art."

"Oh certainly you jest. I know you yanks. At a minimum you look at art if only to ogle at bosoms."

"Sorry. But art never held any interest for me."

"Then why are you in a cemetery? Especially a famous one, so packed with greenery and flowers and deliciously overly-artful headstones and statuary."

Jo looked around as if he had noticed the cemetery for the first time. "I visit cemeteries for the quiet."

I listened and had to agree. The traffic and other sounds of surrounding Paris were muted. A wind blew softly through the trees, the whisper as leaves lightly danced a melody of their own. An old couple chatted on the bench opposite.

"You see," Joe said. "I can hear the dead. The memories of the dead, that is. And, well you see, the memories are strongest around the living and quieter in cemetery wilderness."

I didn't grasp what Jo said, not right away, because I had never before considered that a cemetery could be thought of as a wildness. "What exactly do you mean, you listen to memories?"

"Memories are what are left over when a person dies. I guess some might call that the soul, but try not to think of memories as having identity. Think of memories as a tape recording made of your life, but all recorded from your point of view, and includes all the sights, and sounds, and tastes, and smells, and feelings you experienced and remembered throughout your life. What I hear is all of these recording played together, all mixed, and all combined into new memories from the old."

"Oh, I think I see. You suggest that a person's persona, preserved over the entire course of a person's life is somehow joined to a pool of all such recordings upon death."

Jo's shoulders appeared to sag. "You can't imagine how many times I've tried to explain that concept to people that don't have a clue what I mean. After a while my energy to explain starts to flag. I find myself lately beginning to wonder what the whole point is anyway. So thanks at least for understanding."

I gave him a buddy-like shake of his shoulder. "Buck up," I said. "Have you thought about writing a book."

"I wrote one already. It's with the publisher. They asked me to explain one or another obscure point more clearly. Or to fix a piece of language. That's why I'm in Paris. I'm on vacation, to get away from the publisher for a while and to make some money."

"Oh I'm so sorry. I had no idea that I rubbed salt into a festering wound. But I assure you I know what its like to be on the lamb from a publisher."

Jo smiled and I sensed he was about to relax.

I tapped his arm. "Shall we walk and talk. After all, what's the point of visiting if we don't actually view the place."

We ambled together counter-clockwise around the circle, then turned right up a slight rise. "There," I said, and pointed at a random name. "Jacques Philippe. I believe that's a famous person."

Jo looked where I pointed. "I don't recognize the name. I guess I not all that interested in history. You know. Formal history."

We continued up the rise without speaking. I didn't want to impose on the poor fellow, but his mystic claims had tickled the writer in me.

At the top of the rise Jo stopped and looked around. "Wow, huge!" he said, then he rubbed his chin and added, "At first I thought the next life was reincarnation."

"What?"

Jo crossed his arm. He looked past me, as I recall, not at me, but into the distance. "When I sense someone is about to die I usually experience scenes of a baby afterward. In a bassinet or held in some woman's arms. Sometimes I hover overhead and look down. Sometimes I stand right there in the room. At first I presumed that when you died you came back as a new baby." He looked at me. "So you see why I might mistake a baby as reincarnation."

Jo leaned against a tall thin headstone. Jo's stance blocked my view so I couldn't see who the grave's occupant might be.

I asked, "You no longer think the next life is reincarnation?"

Jo dropped his arm. "Let's walk down there." He started down a narrow side path. Over his shoulder he said, "I visited the places I witnessed in my visions. I visited dozens of such places. Each one should have had a baby, but not one did."

Events of 1977
Joanne Tracy

Book Editor (retired) New York, New York, From a
series of taped interviews.

Jo's first book was what we call a small book, not
in pages, but one that sold fewer than 5,000 copies. At
first fewer copies of course and gave all the appear-
ances of going out of print earlier than I expected,
which would have been bad for me because our
bonuses are based on how well our authors' books sell.

My initial worries were unfounded. No doubt you
heard about the Pope Paul quotation. I mean, of all
people the Pope. In an alleged interview published in Il
Manifesto, the Pope was quoted as saying (I paraphrase
in English), "The 1st Book of Jo a work of pure blas-
phemy."

That was all, that one sentence. Within days the
first printing of his book had sold out, so I ordered a
second printing. I tried to telephone Jo to give him the
news, but his phone had been disconnected. I mailed
him a letter, but that letter was returned marked, "No
forwarding address." I was worried about his welfare
but decided he was merely careless about moving.

The Papal Office quickly stated that the Il Manifesto interview had been a fake. I suppose his denunci-
ation was intended to quiet the masses (pun not
intended).

Johnny Carson next mentioned the book on his
Tonight Show. "What's the world coming to if the Pope
can be misquoted? Maybe Il Manifesto confused Jo
with Job, or even with the Archibald MacLeish play
J.B. or even with a P.B.J."

After the Carson show, The "1st Book of Jo" became mentioned more and more often. The book was reviewed in three southern newspapers in the same week. For the most part, the east and west coasts were more forgiving of the book than was the rest of the country.

I ordered a third printing, then a fourth, then a fifth and sixth, these were all 10,000 book printings.

One of our accountants telephoned me. "We sent a royalty statement and check to Jo Bailey but they were returned as undeliverable." Then he asked, "Do you have a good address for him?"

I apologized and told him I hadn't been able to contact Jo myself.

The company correctly decided to open an escrow account for Jo Bailey and deposited his royalties into it.

Six months after the book was first published, my secretary buzzed me to say there was a Jo Bailey to see me. I was delighted, and had him sent in.

I distinctly recall that Jo Bailey looked bad. His hair was long and uneven, shaggy and he clearly had not shaved. He wore a paint spattered sweat shirt with blue jeans. I suspected he wore sandals too, but I couldn't see his feet.

"Are you okay?" I knew he didn't like me to pry, but I was worried about him.

"I got some threatening phone calls," he said, which surprised me.

"Really?"

"And threatening letters too, so I moved to Costa Rica. I stayed there for three months, but I'm not strong in languages so I left there and went to Kansas."

I sat then he sat and leaned back. Despite his ragtag appearance he seemed relaxed and confident.

"You know," I said. "We were unable to find you so we had to put your royalties into an escrow account."

Jo leaned forward. "Really? How much do I have?"

I had my secretary bring in his paperwork. When I showed the latest royalty report to him his eyebrows rose.

Jo said, "I had no idea my book sold that well."

"We issued 50,000 copies in a twentieth printing. And we licensed the book for French, Spanish, and Japanese translations."

"And nobody has threatened you?"

"Not a soul. We're the publisher, you're the author. If any threatening letter came for you, they would have been turned them over to the police. We try to protect our authors."

Joe asked, "May I keep the royalty statement?"

I nodded.

Jo folded the paper several times small, and slipped the compact result into his jeans pocket. Then he handed me a manila envelope, one I hadn't noticed. "My start on a next book," he told me. "Only a start. I wondered if you might like to handle my second book?"

"I'd like to, but I can't make that decision. I have to get approval for any new project. Do you have an address where I might get in touch with you?"

He pointed at the cover of the envelope. "A P.O. Box."

"No phone yet?"

"No."

"Not even an unlisted number?"

"I don't trust the phone company."

I couldn't think what to say about that, so I nodded. He seemed to take the lull as a sign that the meeting was over.

Jo stood. "Well, thanks, and thanks for the money," he said, and took my hand and said the strangest thing. "Fireworks," he said, as if still talked about money. "Black and red fireworks."

I didn't know how to respond to that so I said, "We'll mail a check to your P.O. Box."

"Thanks," he said. Jo let go of my hand and left.

I scanned the first few pages of the manuscript and found them much more expertly written than had been the first draft of his first book. His first argument actually made sense to me. That pleased me. I began to feel honored to know him.

I gave the envelope to my secretary and asked her to forward his manuscript to my supervising editor. After that I returned to my normal work. We had just started to reprint a classic cookbook.

Events Of 1978
Barry Goodman

On Death Row, San Quentin, California, Assembled
from a series of interviews performed, in the presence
of his lawyer

Yes, I did know the guy that got shot in the post office. I knew him well, even though I never told anyone.

Okay, I'll tell what happened.

His name was Eddy Filbert. He was a high school chum of mine from our days in Los Angeles. We were both in that poetry club. You might not believe that about a crook like me [laughs], but I was a sensitive kid in high school, so was Eddy. Of course I stunk, but Eddy was the teacher's favorite, I mean he could really write poems and he was a bright kid but a bit of a delinquent like me. That is until his step-dad walloped him with a two by four.

For some reason Eddy got into his mind when he turned seventeen that he deserved to drive a car. He drank a few of his step-dad's beers then walked down the neighborhood street, tried one door handle after another, looking for an unlocked car. He found one parked in an apartment house carport, a Jeep. He sat in the driver's seat and hotwired the car. Then he sat there, gunned the engine and didn't go anywhere.

I stood in Eddy's living room with police and Eddy on a stretcher. His step-dad said to the police, "Sure I hit him. Not hard. Not real hard at all. Yeah but twice, once because he hot wired that car, and once because he was too stupid to drive anywhere."

Eddy dropped out of high school. He wasn't right in the head for a year or so after that. He acted like he wanted to go in the front door but always had to enter through the back door and go from room to room. Finally he'd find the front door and turn around and wonder how he got there. And he was never smart afterward, I mean really smart again after that.

Anyway, we drifted apart and together again over the years. But mostly I always kept in touch with him and helped him out with work when I could.

Eddy was married to the sweetest little woman you could ever imagine. Yeah sure she was an ex-stripper from Vegas. But that was only her looks. She was generous and caring to Eddy. But boy was she dumb. She was a woman whose marbles were not lined up in a row. You know the type, the kind who thinks Ben Franklin was the first president [laughs].

They also had a son. He was eight back then and smart as a whip. He played chess and belonged to some group that lived on a mesa, some group of smart people. Eddy lorded over that kid. Eddy never made much money, but somehow he managed to sock away a bit for his boy's college fund. And boy, he believed in his gut that kid of his would do great in college.

So one day Jo tells me he has all these P.O. boxes all over the state and he wants me to collect the mail from them.

"But take someone with you," he says. "A few of those post offices are in bad neighborhoods and I don't want the car left unattended."

"How come you have so many post boxes?" I asked.

"Harder to find me," Jo said. "Nobody can stake out fifty mailboxes and wait for me to show up. And don't let anybody tail you back."

"You got keys for all those boxes?" I ask.

"Most," he says. "One or two you may have to pick a lock or whatever guys like you do. I'm sure you can figure out what to do."

So I phoned Eddy but he's not interested. "Why not?" I asked. "You need the extra money don't you?"

"My boy," he said. "My boy has a chess thing at school. He wants me to go."

"But think of the money," I tell him. "You still don't have enough to send your son to college. And one more job will pay top dollar. I guarantee. Top dollar."

Eddy must have covered the mouthpiece because all I could only hear him mumble. Then he came back and asked, "Are our meals covered?"

"Yeah," I said. "Everything's covered. Meals, rooms, gas, everything. And you get paid too."

He mumbled more, then he said, "My wife says no." And that was that.

I called him back again three times, each time offering him more money. Finally I talked to his wife and told her there was no risk. Finally she said, "Well, ok."

I picked Eddy up on the way out of town. I pulled up in Jo's bullet proof sedan in front of Eddy's apartment building. Winter rain started then stopped then started again. Eddy lived out Third Street in a bad part of town. [laughs] Yeah his wife came down with him and gave him a bag of food for the trip. She wore an apron and a short skirt and boy she had nice gams. Well Eddy kissed her goodbye and got in. Then she leaned in the window.

"Don't you," she said to me serious-like. "Let anything bad happen to my Eddy."

I swore I would protect Eddy and we drove off. We took 101 south to Paso Robles to begin our job. Part of what was in Eddy's bag was a jar of coins. "So I can call her," Eddy once told me. "Every night." A jar of dimes. That's what pay phones cost back then. Or maybe they cost twenty cents. Not quarters yet, I'm certain.

Another thing in the bag was a pint of rum. I think he drank rum because he was in the Coast

Guard for a while until he was kicked out because he lied about graduation from high school. Eddy didn't drink much. But when he was away on a job with me he would leave to call his wife on the nearest pay phone. The he would come back and have exactly one cap-full of rum. Just that much. "To relax me," he said. So the bottle usually lasted for a whole job.

The day Eddy's son was born was summer and hot and Eddy and I were on a job in L.A. Nothing illegal, watched a store across the street from our non-air-conditioned room because the owner was afraid his partner was a thief. Eddy had to leave the room to call his wife so I sat alone with the binocs. Anyway, after a while, Eddy ran in and yelled, "I'm a dad."

I shook his hand and patted him on the back. I suggested we toast. He brought out his pint of rum and emptied one cap-full in each of two bathroom glasses. We toasted the birth of his son with thimbles of rum. [laughs]

Events Of 1986
Wayne Manley

Sheriff Officer (retired), Needles, California Office, His
story as recorded on the last three days of his life

Lester's second trip out Cedar Canyon Road
since his return and the first in sunshine instead of
rain clouds that never seemed to produce rain. I gave
him a guided tour and found out all the interesting
things about his family along the way. For instance
that his sister, my other cousin, had a Ph.D. in physics
and lived in Paris. Or that his mom died of cancer while
he was away in college. He said, "She never let me
know she was sick. Why couldn't she at least let me
know? So I could at least be prepared for her death. Or
maybe find some way to help her live a bit longer."

The car started to bump up and down so I
slowed. "The road was graded recently and re-grav-
eled." I told Lester. Truthfully I was tired of his talk
about death. "But when the grader goes too fast you get
ripples. Hell on a suspension if you take them too fast."

We crested a low hill and below was a wash.
Lester pointed, "What's that?"

A partly buried old red pickup poked up from the
dried red mud in the middle of the wash. "Dumb luck,"
I told him, "Sonny Johnson barely escaped with is life
when the flash flood caught him unaware in that par-
ticular red pickup."

"Was the truck buried with him inside?"

"No. He got out and stood on the roof and waited
there for the flood to ebb."

Lester watched the red top pass by so closely he
could have reached and touched the metal. "He must
have been terribly frightened."

"Either that or he was drunk. More likely from what I know about him."

Lester laughed.

I had to gun the engine to get up the steep incline on the other side and almost ran over one of the common green Mojave rattle snakes that thrived at that narrow altitude.

"That was close," I said.

"What happens if you run over one?"

"Nothing most times," I said, and watched in the rear view to be sure I missed. "But if I'd killed the rattler I'd have to get out and chop its head off and bury the head."

"They're still toxic after their dead?"

"Highly toxic. Dissolves the muscles."

We cruised up and passed the rock house perched up on a low hill to our left. As I rounded its dirt drive, a new looking pickup and a dusty station wagon came into view.

"Damn," I said to Lester. "I forgot I was supposed check on him for Mrs. Dodson's. You mind if we stop?"

"No problem," he said. "I have extra heart medicine for Mr. Aloshapman and need to check his blood pressure. He can wait."

When I turned off my truck's engine the cab made noise like metal cooling, but I knew whole truck was actually heating. Mid-August meant the mercury was over 100 at noon. The air was bone dry and not a whisper of wind with the grace to cool. Dust stirred by our boots fell immediately back to ground as if on the moon. Hats were mandatory. My trooper's hat had a wide brim and Lester wore a woven straw hat he claimed was cooler than mine.

The rock house had been hand built by persons unknown in the late 1800s. The house was set back from the road on a slight hill. No front door had been installed yet, so we stepped right inside. Two guys in sleeveless t-shirts jacked up a center roof support with one of those red Hi-Rise jacks. No roof was up yet, the hard blue of the desert sky above and as hot inside as out.

"Which one of you is the guy that's moving in?" I asked them.

They paused in their work and wiped their hands on their pants. The taller of the two, a thickly muscled man with brightly tattooed arms, reached to shake my hand. "Neither of us," he said, and we shook. "He's in Needles picking up rolls of tin for the roof. We're two of his body guards."

That gave me a start. I'd never known anyone with body guards before and found the idea somewhat distasteful.

"You fellows should wear hats," Lester told them. "To protect you from the sun." He reached out his hand to shake too. "I'm Doc Manley, but you can call me Lester. Everyone does."

I glanced around out of habit while Lester talked and spotted shoulder holsters hung from nails on the wall with semi-automatics in them. By habit my own hand moved to my holster. "You got permits for those," I asked.

The shorter body guard stepped over and pulled out his wallet. "Sure do," he said. He extracted two folded yellow permits and handed them to me.

They looked official to me with embossed seals and all. I shook my head. "These are from Los Angeles county," I told him. "Which one of you is Elmo Jones and which is Tom Mandonly?"

The shorter body guard said, "I'm Elmo." He gestured with his thumb. "That's Tom."

Outside another car pulled up and stopped.

I glanced outside but couldn't see a car from my angle. "You have fifteen days to get permits from Needles," I handed the permits back.

"We'll be gone in fifteen days," Elmo said. He gestured toward the doorway with his head. "That's our boss."

"See that you are," I told him. "Either that or get local permits."

Lester and I walked outside. A middle-aged man untied rolls of tin. "You the owner?" I asked him.

"Yeah," he said, and casually slipped off his leather work gloves.

He looked to be a man in his mid- to late-forties. He was dusty but casually dressed in expensive looking city clothes. His watch, a gold Rolex, convinced me at once that he had money. We shook hands and I introduced him to Lester.

He took Lester's hand to shake then paused. He looked at Lester hard and said, "You'll pull in front of a semi truck. You won't sense anything coming. Headlights will suddenly appear out of darkness and hit your car. The collision will kill you instantly."

"What are you?" I asked. "One of those LA fortune tellers?"

"Sorry." he said to me, and let Lester's hand drop. "At least this one was free."

I noticed Lester looked a little shaken.

The man shook my hand a second time. "I'm Jo Bailey. Maybe you've heard about me?"

I had to confess I hadn't. "Nope." I said. Back then, you see, I had no idea who Mr. Bailey was.

Lester said to him, "The real Jo Bailey?"

Mr. Bailey nodded.

Lester said to me, "I think I need to sit its cold air for a while."

"Sure," I said, and handed him my car keys. I didn't think anything was amiss until later. I turned back to face Mr. Bailey.

"Why do you need body guards?"

"I won't need them. Nobody knows I'm I here at the rock house."

"You a crook or something?" I confess I felt a qualm of guilt because I didn't check him out for Mrs. Dodson.

"No," Mr. Bailey laughed. "I write books and, well, some people don't like what I say."

"What do you write?"

"Religious books. But I say things that make other people angry. So when I'm in a big town I need body guards."

"Yeah," I said, but I really didn't understand. Not then anyway. "Religion can stir up a real hornet's nest."

"That's right," Mr. Bailey said. "But surrounded by wilderness," he waved his hand in a sweep indicating the desert surrounding the rock house. "Nobody knows where I am, so I'm safe." He pulled a red bandana from his back pocket and wiped his head.

"I'm Wayne Manley, the sheriff in these parts," I said. We shook hands a third time. More his doing than mine. "You plan to retain any guns?"

"Don't need them," Mr. Bailey smiled. "Anyway, I'm Jo Bailey." He paused like he expected me to know him.

"Well try to stay out of trouble Mr. Bailey and we'll get along fine."

But then he reached and lightly touched my arm. No spark or anything magic. Just a light touch. Then he said, "A chicken." I noticed he had closed his eyes. "Far in the future. Vague. A chicken with its foot caught in the crack of a table. The caught bird flaps its wings in panic and sends dishes scattering and breaking." Then he lifted his light touch from my arm.

"Nice to meet you Mr. Bailey," I said to him. He opened his eyes and looked at me. "You take care," I told him and turned away. I was more convinced he was a harmless crackpot than anything else.

I returned to the car, cool because Lester had been idling the engine and had the air on full blast. I drove off and noticed Mr. Bailey in the mirror telling his body guards to unload the truckload of tin.

I delivered Lester to Mr. Aloshapman where he did his doctor stuff. Then on the way back Lester told me all about Mr. Bailey, and the more I heard the more I realized how rude Mr. Bailey had been to tell Lester how he would die.

"I've read Jo Bailey's books," Lester told me. "And over and over he gives evidence that his predictions of death are correct. If you read his books I'm sure you'd feel the same way. So I hope you'll understand," I felt him look at me. "If I left my car in the shop and didn't drive any more."

I looked at him and despite the sunset dimness I could see he was shaking. "No problem," I told him. "You're family, so of course I'll be happy to drive you anywhere you need."

That finally seemed to calm Lester so we talked of other things on the rest of the trip back. Mostly, as I recall, his ex again.

Events of 1975
Paul Langdon

Adapted from his essays "Paris Waits."

The path was too narrow to walk beside him, so I followed. "What about the women. You said you saw mothers with babies."

A few paces in, he stopped. "I opened some wounds," he said.

I moved up behind Jo. "What do you mean?"

Jo looked around as if he watched something that wasn't there. "I recently witnessed a death about to happen and afterward had a vision of a young mother, possibly in her teens. She held a baby on the front steps of a walk-up. I recognized the place. The apartment was on the corner of the same city in which I was, Oakland as I recall."

I squeezed between a monolith and the statue of an angel so that I could move around in front of Jo.

"I noted the street name and the address." Jo continued. He ignored me completely. "I went there. The corner was the same. The address was the same. I knocked on the door. A middle aged woman answered the door. Pardon me, I told her, do you have a teen aged daughter? She stared at me. Maybe, I asked, with a new baby?"

Jo blinked and his eyes focused on me. "How dare you, she yelled at me. Her baby she told me, was shot and killed in its crib by a bullet from down the street twenty years ago. Killed by a boy angry about drug money. Her mother, she told me, died sixteen years ago and she had lived alone since then."

I asked Jo, "So what baby did you see?"

"My vision was of a teen-aged woman hold a baby in her arms. A man from inside the door yelled to her, 'Hey Tracy when you going to fix dinner?' So her name," Jo looked at me again. "The teenager's name was Tracy. So there on the steps I asked the woman at the door if her daughter's name was Tracy. 'Yes,' she said. Her middle name was Tracy. And asked me how I knew that. I could see in her face that I had opened a wound that had been closed for all these years. 'Please go,' she said, after an awkward silence when I couldn't think of anything to add. So I left."

Frankly, I was a bit annoyed with myself for going along with Jo. His story didn't appear to me to go anywhere. "You mean the mother was reborn, grew into a teenager and gave birth to that baby?"

"Yes but not in our present world. Not reborn. Not reincarnated."

I crossed my arms. "If not reincarnation, then what?"

"Memories. We play back as memories. We don't really live again."

"But where are these memories?" I gestured with my arms to indicate the sky. "In the air? In the ether? In the space between the stars?"

Jo hung his head. "I don't know. I haven't figured that out yet."

I felt sorry for the confused mystic. "Buck up," I told him. "You have plenty of time to solve your problems. Look. On such a fine warm day, let's say we actually search for a famous name? Maybe we find a famous musician."

We walked for a while, then I said to him, "Maybe those memories are in other dimensions."

"No," he said. "Definitely not other dimensions. That's science fiction. Cheap ideas from cheap books. Not thoughtful or informed writing at all."

I crossed my arms and glared at him.

He noticed my discomfort and ask, "Did I say something wrong?"

"I'm sorry," I told him. "I should have told you from the start that I write science fiction for a living."

He grinned sheepishly, clearly embarrassed. "I meant that terms like other dimensions don't fit with traditional religious dialogue."

"But recorded and replayed memories do?"

"Well yes. Because replayed is more like reincarnation."

"But you yourself said, these babies don't appear in our world, in our reality."

Jo didn't reply. I walked up and stood next to him. We stood in front of a low, flat topped sarcophagus. Spread over its top were dozens of framed photographs of Jim Morrison. I said, "Must be Jim Morrison's grave."

"Who's Jim Morrison?" Jo asked. He looked down and rubbed dirt with the sole of his shoe.

I laughed. "He's with the Doors, you know, the band."

Jo gazed at the photographs and I could see from his bland expression that the images meant nothing to him. He had jammed his hands into his pockets and stood with a slouch, shoulders drooped. I stood silently with him for a moment then asked, "Can you tell when I'm going to die?" I asked then immediately regretted asking.

He glanced sideways at me and said, "I don't do that for free anymore."

"What do you mean?"

"I'm not proud," he said, without looking at me. "Sometimes I'm ashamed. But to know when someone will die can be worth money. I mean a lot of money."

That made perfect sense. I would think that people of power might profit from knowledge of when a key individual will die. I crossed my arms and turned to face him. "How much is a lot?"

He turned to face me at last, but stayed slouched with his hands still in his pockets. "I probably shouldn't say," he said, and then stood straight and looked around. "Let's find someplace more open, so I can be certain nobody will eavesdrop."

Events of 1977
Joanne Tracy

Book Editor (retired) New York, New York, From a
series of taped interviews.

Not more than a week later, my supervising editor called me into his office to discuss Jo Bailey's book.
His meeting seemed abnormally quick which, I
thought, boded well for Jo's second book.

I entered his office, a starkly bare room but for
his desk and two chairs. Sunlight leaked through
partly drawn curtains. I was startled to find one of the
corporation's lawyers there. "Hi Al," I said to my boss.
"What's with the lawyer?"

"Have a seat," Al said.

I sat and introduced myself to the lawyer.

"Pleased to meet you," he said. "I'm Jason Cum-
mings, with libel and slander."

On the desk I noticed a thick folder, perhaps six
or eight inches thick. "What's that?"

Al nodded at the folder. "Threats," he said.

"Threats to Jo Bailey?"

"Only about 10 percent," Jason said. "The other
90 percent are threats against you, the other editors
and the corporation."

I was stunned. I had no idea we had been threatened too.

"Remember," Al said to me. "About four months
ago we had that bomb scare and had to evacuate the
building?"

"Yes. But the bomb was a dud."

"Well that bomb was first threatened in one of
these letters.

"My god. Why didn't you tell me?"

Al paused with arched fingers and looked hard at me. "We didn't want to bother you with anything serious. Better to leave you to your cookbooks."

I sat there stunned and couldn't think of a sensible word to say. But I had never been pandered to so directly and obviously before.

"We have to decline Jo Bailey's next book," the lawyer said.

Al looked at the lawyer then at me. "I want you to let Jo know our decision."

I didn't answer right away. The magnitude of the risk was too much for me to accept right away. I felt a bit sick. That afternoon, I dictated the necessary letter to my secretary and had her mail that notice to Jo Bailey's P.O. Box.

Not less than two weeks later, the police telephoned me.

"You Joanne Tracy?"

"Yes." The voice on the phone had that hard edged gruffness that seemed genuinely police-like and official.

"You sent a letter to Jo Bailey at his P.O. Box?"

"Yes."

"Any word from Jo Bailey since then?"

"No, I can't say I've been contacted at all."

"Well a man jimmied Jo Bailey's P.O. Box, we suspect to steal his checks."

"Hmm. That's right, we sent his royalty checks to that address and recently sent him a letter turning down his second book."

"Well the box was stuffed full of envelopes."

"Not from us, surely, we would only have sent him a one or two checks at most."

"Are you sure?"

"Positive."

"That's interesting. We'll have to look into that."

"Is that all?"

"No. Nothing to do with you, but someone shot and killed the man that broke into the P.O. Box. We suspect the killer thought the man was Jo Bailey."

"Is that so?" I asked. I recalled the stack of threats the lawyer showed me two weeks before.

"Yeah. That's so. So have you heard from him?"

"I haven't, but leave your name and number with my secretary and I will let you know when, and if, I hear from him."

The police officer thanked me. I transferred him to my secretary and leaned back to think.

So what happened to Jo Bailey? I only know what you know. I heard about the speech at the Greek Theater in Berkeley, California. But then, I suppose, everyone knows about that. He never contacted me again. We no longer mailed checks to his P.O. box once they came back marked "No room in box." We set up an escrow account for him again. The last time I asked, which was some years ago, there was over two million dollars in that account.

Events Of 1978
Barry Goodman

On Death Row, San Quentin, California, Assembled
from a series of interviews performed, in the presence
of his lawyer

Well the job of collecting mail from post office boxes went from good to bad. The first was in a post office that had moved. We took an hour to find the new one and by then that one was closed too. The next post office box was easy, but the one after that was empty except for a note. The note said, "Box full. Collect mail at the counter."

Of course they wouldn't give anything to us because neither of us was Jo. I had to telephone Jo and he faxed something to the post office so they finally agreed to give us the mail.

After a week that should have been three days, we got to the first post office with a missing key. We stopped in Barstow late. The evening was dark and the counter inside was closed. Somehow I'd imagined until then that I might get a duplicate key from somewhere.

Under rain and darkness, the post office was on a main street; no parking near. Tricky parking because there was a popular bar across the street. I ended up parked a block away under some trees that dropped heavy thumps of rain on the roof of the car.

"What should I do?" Eddy asked. He knew we didn't have a key.

"Look through the glove box," I told him.

He did and found a screwdriver. "Should work," he said, and got out of the car. Those were the last words he ever spoke.

Like I said I had to park a block away, so I watched Eddy in the rear view, walk down the sidewalk and vanish inside. The rain fell heavier, became more of a storm. That song from Hair was on the radio. You know, the one about, "What a piece of work is man." I watched Eddy walk and listened to that song, well that song made me laugh [laughs].

I don't know if you ever wondered about last words. I do a lot; with my being on death row and all. "Should work," seemed weak to me. I always regret that one. Others would break your heart [lawyer touches his arm] but I guess I shouldn't talk about those. I been thinking about mine. Thinking a lot actually. I think I'll say, "Defoe, you shouldn't have killed Eddy." Just that. Simple.

Anyway, back to Eddy. Like I said, I sat in the car. I had quit smoking by then but the rain and all made me miss cigarettes a little. So I fidgeted and waited. After a little while there were several bright flashes in the post office windows and pops that I recognized right away as gun shots. "Eddy?" I think I asked myself aloud. I waited and watched in the mirror. I hoped to spot Eddy come out of the door. A shadow come out, bent over, and hurried the other way away from the car. But Eddy never came out. I waited until police cars appeared, then I drove off.

I didn't want to involve Mr. Bailey in anything bad but I had to let him know what happened. As I drove, I looked for a pay phone in the rain. I imagined Eddy trapped in that post office. Trapped with a shooter and no place to run. I began to wonder if maybe he was shot because he pried open the box. But that didn't make any sense. Or maybe he was shot because someone wanted to shoot Jo. That made more sense. Anyway I quickly found a pay phone outside the Greyhound station. I pulled over and called Jo. I had to use Eddy's dimes.

"Oh no," Jo said. "You'd better come right back."

I found out later that the cops came by Eddy's house. "He was shot by persons unknown while stealing checks from a PO box," they said to his wife. "He died quickly." I don't see what good saying "quickly" does anyone. But that's the cops for you.

Yeah his wife was pissed at me. I mean wouldn't you be too if you promised what I promised? I mean man, I keep kicking myself.

Events Of 1986
Wayne Manley

Sheriff Officer (retired), Needles, California Office, His
story as recorded on the last three days of his life

Back in the office I found Andy still in the office. I
told him about Mr. Bailey at the old rock house on
Cedar Canyon Road. Andy stopped typing and looked
at me.

"You don't mean the Jo Bailey, the religious guy,
do you?"

"You know him?"

"Sure. I expect lots of folks do."

I approached Andy's desk. "Look," I told him.
"Keep Jo Bailey secret. He's not safe out there and you
might risk harm to him if you let anyone know he's
there."

"Okay, okay," Andy said. "You got my word."

I accepted his word, although I shouldn't have.

I glared at Andy, and then said, "Lester got a
pinched nerve in his leg so can't drive for a few months.
I'll give him a lift when I can, but I expect you to help
too and so will my dad."

"Okay," Andy said.

You see, I didn't believe what Mr. Bailey claimed.
But Lester believed, hook line and sinker. "When Jo
Bailey says you're going to die," he told me. "You can
wager on my death and win. That's how I will die.
Blind-sided by a truck while driving my car."

"So we won't let your drive."

"You think you can cheat fate?"

"Ain't fate I'd be cheating. I'd be cheating Mr.
Bailey."

Lester strapped a leg brace to his left leg and foot and left in place for months. The brace was made of flesh colored wraps and metal side uprights which he wore outside his pants. Between me, my dad, Andy and Maggie the waitress from Juicy's restaurant we managed to keep Lester from any need to drive his car. Of course Dad and I were the only ones to know the real reason.

After a week or so, Lester asked me to put a special sign on 95, the main road through town. I got the county supervisors to agree with my logic, about kids and school, of course not about Lester. The signs were put up and trucks were limited to 25 through town. That made the local businesses happy too because slow trucks tended to stop in town.

Early one morning that autumn, Lester confessed to me quietly over breakfast, "I've been really tempted to drive. When someone calls hurt or sick and I can't get a ride right away. You know, I actually sat in the car and idled the engine a few minutes yesterday. So I need you to do me a favor."

"What's that?" I asked him. He appeared genuinely worried.

He leaned close and whispered, "Take my drivers license away. Please."

I patted him on his back and said, "Okay." But of course nothing was that simple, I had to make up a crime which I report to the DMV in Sacramento. Then they cancelled his driver's license, and not in a nice way.

Life went on like that for next few months. Lester wanted me to impound his car. Then he wanted me to make sure my dad never parked his car with the keys in the ignition. Little things, sure, but they all added up to an ongoing fear of death. Hit by a truck, but never told where or when.

A week before Christmas I got a call from old Mr. Aloshapmen the man with the bad heart who lived up the road from Mr. Bailey.

"I drove by the rock house last night, on my way back from Needles, and there wasn't no lights on. I always see lights on. And that funny jeep was out front. Just no lights. I didn't want to check myself because I not brave in the middle of the night, so I thought I'd call you."

I promised to head out there first thing in the morning and that seemed to be good enough. But I felt uneasy. I decided to grab a quick dinner at the Juicy's restaurant, my usual steak with mashed potatoes. Juicy's is like a home away from home, with checkered red on white naugahyde table cloths and big white dishes. I must have appeared uneasy because the wait-ress, Maggie, newly pregnant, asked me, "You okay, sheriff?"

"Fine Maggie. I got a call about the rock house but I can investigate in the morning."

"The rock house where Jo Bailey lives?"

"You know about Mr. Bailey?"

"Sure," she said. "Everyone does. Andy told me months ago."

I felt jarred by the news and betrayed. I felt in my bones that something bad had happened to Mr. Bailey. I stood quickly and dragged the table cloth with me. "Shit Maggie," I told her. "I gotta get out there."

I started for the door then turned back to Maggie. "If you see Andy," I said, loud enough for everyone in the restaurant to hear. "Tell him he's fired."

Events of 1975
Paul Langdon

Adapted from his essays "Paris Waits."

Jo led the way and we soon found ourselves among wide rows of low grave sites. Wide open with a clear range of view. There were only a few people present and they were at the far other end.

"Okay," Jo said.

I stopped and faced him.

He looked at me with an earnest frown, "You have to promise to never write about what I tell you. At least while I'm alive. I only say so because you said you were a writer."

"You have my word," I said.

Jo looked around, not so much to see if anyone listened in, but maybe more to buy some time to think. After a moment he shrugged and began. "An Arabian group, all wealthy. I met them in a hotel suite, you know, a big room with lots of rooms inside. I was asked to evaluate two men. I was to receive two million dollars each if I was correct. I was told to first look at a middle aged man in an expensive white robe. I visualized him with vague death in the far future, many years away and told them that."

Jo looked away then, as if he watched the distant grave visitors. "Then they brought in another man. The man was handcuffed and wore a tattered black robe. I assumed he was a prisoner. They asked me to view the man as the second one. I looked at him and witnessed his head chopped off with a long curved sword. His death was near, perhaps hours away. I told them the prisoner would be beheaded within hours. That seemed to please the main guys, but the guy in the black robe yelled at me. Told me he was innocent. Told me he wasn't a prisoner. He was a waiter. He shouted his innocence as they dragged him away."

Jo started to walk off then stopped and turned back to me again. "You see they planned to kill the waiter as a test. If I could predict the waiter's death they would trust that the guy in the white robes would live a long time."

I asked, "Did they kill him?"

"They must have or I wouldn't have foreseen that outcome."

"And they paid you?"

"They mailed a check. I always had them send checks to my P.O. boxes. I never want to carry big checks or lots of cash."

"I can see that. If you did, you'd become a target of a different kind."

"You won't print anything I told you?"

"Not while you still alive."

He appeared to relax then. "Earning lots of money takes a toll."

I walked up to him and clapped him on the shoulder. "I can see that."

I noticed a dozen or so folk gathered around a grave near the end of our row. "Hey. Let's head down there and see what's up. Maybe somebody famous."

We walked down without further conversation about his job. At the grave I peered at the photo on top. "Edith Piaf's grave."

"Who's that?"

I swear, I'd never met anyone who knew less about music than Jo Bailey. "She's a famous cabaret and record singer. She sang 'Milord' and 'La Vie En Rose'."

Jo shrugged. I noticed the few French people who watched us, frowned at Jo.

Jo looked at his watch. "I have to leave," he said. "I have an appointment in town."

"The same type of job?"

He smiled because I had saved his secret. "Yeah," he said. "The same type of job."

I walked with him toward the exit. Near the arched entry he stopped and said, "I'll read you for free."

I stopped and looked at him. "I'm not sure I want to know anymore."

But he looked at me anyway. There was nothing special about his gaze, maybe his eyes were a bit more open, and maybe his brow was a bit more furrowed. But on the whole he looked more like he had simply seen a pimple on my face, one he wanted to study.

"Rain," he said. "Very distant."

I had been holding my breathe. I breathed out.

"I see two black umbrellas and hand drawn hearts everywhere, black outlines of hearts. But no death, not then or for a good while after."

I thanked Jo and walked out the gate with him.

"A two million dollar gift," he said.

"And worth every pence."

He laughed and shook my hand.

Jo left me once we exited the cemetery. He dashed down the Metro and vanished from my life. He didn't look back or wave. He turned away and fled down the steps. "A pence is not a penny," were his parting words.

Later that same summer I met and married my wife Ellen. We moved back to London, where I worked with national health to earn money while I waited for my books to sell.

Many years past. Mine has been a fulfilling life, not so much from my writing, more from my family.

After that I lost track of Jo. I noticed his first book in a book store and bought a copy. I tried to read a few pages, but found them preachy and apologetic.

His second book was more maturely written, but I still could not accept his far fetched ideas.

A few years back we, as a family, finally took a another summer off together, my first full summer since my youth. The boys were in their teenage years and had a great time on the trip. One day, while in Paris, we decided to visit Pere Laschaise cemetery. The day, as I recall, was chilly and threatened rain, but we went regardless.

We found Jim Morrison's grave easily, clearly marked on a tiny map handed out at the gate. His grave was cordoned off with metal barricades and lightly crowded. I didn't find much to look at, but my wife and sons were enthralled.

As we later walked away from the grave I stopped at a marble urn full of flowers on another grave. I waited for my wife to stop talking to our sons. She stopped and turn to look at me. Then I told her what Jo had described years earlier.

The two boys wandered away to hunt. They looked under and around all the graves surrounding Jim Morrison's and kept discovering hidden graffiti. Mostly hearts, mostly outlines of hearts.

Then rain began to seriously fall. My wife and I raised our umbrellas. Holding our two black umbrellas gave me another chill because of the memory. We called to our sons to come get their umbrellas. But they ignored us as teenage boys do.

I realized I had lived the same future that Jo had described.

"Jo. Jo Bailey," I said. "You recall I told you I met him, once, long ago. Well back then he described a future to me. I didn't so much believe him. . . ."

"But you do believe him?" My wife completed my thought.

"Yeah," I laughed. "The best two million dollars I ever spent."

My wife laughed a puzzled laugh and put her arm around me. "You know," she said. "Perhaps you should write up what happened. I would certainly like to hear about your strange encounter with him."

"Maybe," I said. "Or maybe I'll write up an article for the London Times."

My wife laughed. I don't believe she took me seriously.

The boys continued to explore wet cemetery. I would have joined them had I been years younger. I wondered as I watched them if I was a memory. A recording of myself lost in the gulf between stars. Replaying over and over, trapped in a loop I could never detect.

I looked at my wife. "Can other dimensions exist? You know, with string theory?"

My wife took my hand, smiled at me and nodded.

I squeezed her hand. And then we walked back together silently through a wilderness in the rain, the mood inevitably shattered by the arrival of our sons

Events of 1977
Joanne Tracy

Book Editor (retired) New York, New York, From a
series of taped interviews.

Monday was my last day as an editor exactly six years to the day after I first met Jo Bailey. I was engaged to be married for my second time and we planned to move to San Francisco. I parked as usual in the firm's underground garage. Since Jo's success I was given one of the rare parking spots, a huge deal in a city like New York. I always arrived early and so the garage was never crowded. A big mistake.

I locked my car door when someone grabbed me from behind in a bear hug. "Don't scream," he whispered into my ear. I was too surprised to scream. At first I thought Carl McFredricks from accounting had grabbed me. He always pulled jokes like that. Once he put a whoopee cushion in the break room; once I opened one of those fake cans of nuts with cloth covered spring inside. But no sooner had I relaxed into the bear hug that another man stepped in front of me and I knew at once this wasn't a joke.

The second man was dark haired with a grizzly beard. He smiled and his teeth appeared broken or oddly uneven, and when he spoke I smelled garlic. "Shut up," he said. Of course I hadn't said anything. The man behind me let go and slipped a bag over my head. Then they tied my hands behind me and that's when I finally became frightened. The bag must have been burlap because sneezed. I had never thought much about death before then, but suddenly in the dark like that I remembered that someone had been shot in a post office. I didn't want to be shot and didn't know if these were the same people or not.

They made me sit in the back seat of a car, then drove. I had to sit sideways to get comfortable, because my hands were tied behind. I tried to push the hood away from my nose with my tongue but failed. The fabric was course but didn't smell like anything, maybe a new smell.

The car pulled out of the garage, then drove for a long time into the countryside. I asked over and over where we were going, but both men remained dead silent throughout the whole drive. They listened the radio for a while, more news stories about starvation in Ethiopia and the assassination of Indira Gandhi. Then, without comment, they shut the radio off. I must have nodded off because when the car finally stopped I woke up when the car door next to my head opened.

They took me inside a room that sounded hollow, a place with a hard, probably cement floor. They sat me in a metal chair and tied with a coarse rope. They ran the rope around my middle two or three times then tied my arms down to the arms of the chair. I felt my arms start to shake; I couldn't will them to stop. My mouth felt dry.

I don't know how long I sat there. I think they must have left the room. After maybe an hour or so, I smelled coffee and the men walked in. "Where do we find Jo Bailey?" the gruff voiced one asked.

I tried to convince them I didn't know any Jo Bailey. I would never betray a fine man like Jo Bailey to thugs. But they didn't seem to buy my reason. "I'm a woman," I said. "A big publishing house like that would never let a woman be an editor. Use your heads. I mean that's a man's world. How could I be anything other than a secretary? I want to be an editor, sure. Who doesn't? A cold day in hell before that happens."

We went back and forth like that for a long while, maybe an hour. But I kept to my guns and never let on that I was Jo's editor. I didn't want these men to find Jo. Finally they sounded like they lost enthusiasm for their questions. Then, just as suddenly, they stopped asking. I hadn't heard them leave, so I thought they still hung around. I asked for water, then for a bathroom, but couldn't get them to answer.

Anyway, I finally believed they were gone so I struggled to get out off the ropes. The knot was sloppier than I expected because, once I started the ropes seemed to fall off. Once free, I pulled that itchy hood off and found myself in round room with a really tall ceiling. I mean really high with birds in the rafters. I walked to the only door which opened easily and swung out. I stood outside in the sunshine of late afternoon. I had been held in the grain silo of an abandoned farm.

I stood there amazed. I felt lucky to be alive. I spread my arms and spun in place. Birds peppered bare tree limbs. A hundred or more black birds. I could have sworn they remained still; watched me and waited like I did. I felt so relieved and good in that moment, that I let out a whoop and clapped. The birds took flight all at once. A thousand black birds took flight over the abandoned farm. A thousand black birds with red wings wheeled overhead in a symphonic fireworks display. An explosion of life that perfectly echoed how I felt in that moment. Alive, but unfortunately two hours long walk away from the nearest phone.

Later, after I got back, the police got involved. The police didn't have enough clues to even begin to search for the two men. The sketch made of the driver didn't match any mug shots. I didn't go back to work for three weeks and then did so only to quit my job.

I tried to write a novel about my kidnapping, but I'm not really a writer so the effort didn't go anywhere. And besides I think I was still too afraid to have those men find out I had lied to them. But that was long ago, and well, with the formation of the Church of Jo and all, I feel more confident.

I'm not so afraid anymore. And between you and me, I think my publisher was a fool to pass up Jo's second book.

Events Of 1978
Barry Goodman

On Death Row, San Quentin, California, Assembled
from a series of interviews performed, in the presence
of his lawyer

The second event you asked me about was the Greek Theater. I was there too, but you might know that because of the news footage, because I had a pretty distinctive beard then.

Jo was one of a dozen or so religious people who spoke there. As I recall most had to do with crystals and stuff like that. He was up last so I waited with him backstage and listened to the others. Finally his turn arrived.

I don't recall a lot of what he said. He spoke for ten or so minutes. A couple times the audience clapped. Then he started to talk really weird stuff, "I've inhabited aliens too. Creatures from other planets."

Then an older man, maybe in his 50's, with wild black hair and a beard, stood up in the back row and yelled, "Death to heathens," or something like that. You'd know cuz of the news footage back then. The man pulled a pistol and shot at the stage.

I may look fat to you, but back then I was pure muscle. I could move like lightening if I had to and that time I had to. I rushed out and grabbed Jo in a body hug, to place me between him and the shooter.

I hustled him off stage and protected him from the panicked people tried to squeeze around us. I didn't expect to be hit because, well, a pistol like that, from that far away can't be aimed worth shit.

At some point, still back stage, I felt Jo relax and began to talk, so I had to lift and carry him. What he said then was so damn odd that I wrote everything down after. [Lawyer passes him a tablet of paper]

"I see a woman and her daughter in front of a grave. They are dressed in black, both of them. They put flowers on the grave. They weep. I can't see the name on the grave."

You gotta understand, Jo was in my arms, but traveled somewhere else to visit folks. But each time he seemed to travel to a different place.

Joe continued to speak in my arms, his mouth behind my back. "A young woman on stage in a gymnasium. She is dressed like a graduating senior. She says, 'Mostly I credit my dad. Shot down in the Greek Theater that Sunday afternoon long ago. His essays, his lessons, his wisdom, carried me to where I am, and will, I am certain, carry me beyond.'

"I am on a stage over the reflecting pool in Washington, D.C. Thousands and thousands of people surround the pool. The woman next to me on the stage speaks. Music plays somewhere, rhythmic but soft. She holds up her hands to quiet the crowds so she can speak. She resembles the girl in the Gymnasium only older."

I laid Jo down in the back seat of the car. As I let go, his eyes seemed to focus and he said, "He died. I don't know who."

Just before I quit my job with Jo, I found out he had taken care of Eddy's family. He'd given Eddy's wife a half-million bucks tax free. And, if that wasn't enough, he set up an endowment for Eddy's kid, enough to send him to the best college.

Which brings me the reason I'm in here. Later, much later when I no longer worked for Jo, I found out as a favor from a guy I knew inside stir that the shooter was the same guy that had shot Eddy. His name was Defoe Scallody and he was in Folsom prison convicted of shooting that man at the Greek. I guess they didn't know about the post office. My guy on the inside had overheard that Defoe guy brag about shooting someone at the post office in Barstow. So I knew that was him.

About five years ago, Defoe was paroled. He never paid for Eddy so I found him and when I did I was surprised because he was older than I expected. I found him in a real dive; Sophie's Bar, on South Grand in downtown L.A.

I wore doubled sunglasses, you know twice as dark. I took them off as the door closed behind me to the bar, that way I could be already 90% used to the darkness. Only one bartender stood behind the bar and that Defoe guy sat on a bar stool half way back. I walked up to the bar and noticed that Defoe paid no attention to me. The bartender, middle-aged and bald with a pronounced pot belly, asked what I wanted so I handed him a hundred bucks and softly said to him, "Stock the back room for say ten minutes or so."

He smiled at me without a missed beat. "Well when you make up your mind," he said. "Shout. I'll be in back sorting stock."

I waited for the bartender to disappear in the back. As the swinging door swung shut I walked over and sat one stool away from Defoe. He still ignored me, and still was bent over a tumbler of what looked like whiskey. Both hands cupped the glass.

I cocked my gun and set that heavy metal instrument on the bar. The sound caught Defoe's attention. He looked at me. When he did, I remembered the look of the man in the Greek. Defoe had the same dark hair and wild eyes but his beard was different, close-cut and gray.

"Who are you?" he asked. I could smell garlic and whiskey on his breath.

"You shot my friend Eddy in the post office in Barstow"

"So?"

"You shot a man in the Greek Theater in Berkeley and you were in Folsom for a while for that one."

"So what."

I picked up the gun and pointed death at him. I used a forty-five revolver then and which looked like a small cannon in my hand.

One of Defoe's eyebrows rose. Just one. "You know Jo Bailey?" he asked.

"I worked for him."

"You tell Jo Bailey," he said, and smiled. His teeth looked rotten. "You tell Jo Bailey that I killed his mother."

That surprised me. I had to compute in my head how old Jo was and how old Defoe looked. Possible sure, but I said, "So?"

"You can kill me," his smile faded. "But there's seven of us. Six plus me. We're on a mission. Tell Jo Bailey that for me. Tell Jo Bailey we're on a mission to kill him."

"Tell him yourself," I told him and smiled. "He visits the dead you know."

Defoe turned away then. I guess he had his say and that was that. He turned away and bent over his drink again. Bent over like that, he resembled the shadow that night. The hunched over shadow that ran the other way away from the car parked too far away from the post office.

I shot him the same way he'd shot Eddy. Twice in the stomach. I set the gun on the bar with my prints all over it. I turned and walked out into the bright sunlight so that Defoe would die alone.

And that's why I'm on death row. I murdered the man that murdered my friend.

They'll give me the needle some day. I suppose I deserve to die. No I don't suppose nothing. I do deserve to die. Nobody should have to die the way Eddy died, not even his killer. That's a bad way to go, with your insides on fire and the certain knowledge you're about to die. Damn those cops. Damn them anyway for their lie to Eddy's wife. He didn't die fast like they told her. No, he died slow and alone and in pain.

Events Of 1986
Wayne Manley
Sheriff Officer (retired), Needles, California Office, His
story as recorded on the last three days of his life

The drive to the rock house ordinarily takes an
hour in daylight. But at night, with all the blind cor-
ners on that dirt road, the trip took an hour or more. I
arrived at the rock house at exactly five minutes before
ten.

Like Mr. Aloshapmen had told me, the rock
house was dark and a Land Rover pickup was parked
out front. The last quarter of a moon that night made
the rock house appear even darker.

I knocked on the front door and waited. The
house remained totally silent. The front door was
locked so I worked my way around toward the back
and tried to see in through the windows with my flashlight. The windows were all curtained. At the side of the
house, the side away from the outhouse, a window had
two bullet holes. They were large holes with minimal
cracks, the kind that might be made by a high caliber
rifle. I touched the glass; plastic which explained why
the window hadn't shattered.

I turned and shined my light back out into the
field. No reflections from scope lenses so I figured there
was nobody there. Just the same, I cupped the flashlight with my hand and made my way back to my
truck.

Despite hot days, the desert can be bitter cold at
night. I picked up the radio mike which felt like ice in
my hand. "Andy," I called. "You in the office?"

"You fired me."

"Get over yourself," I must have still sounded pissed but felt ashamed. "Round up Lester and drive him up to the rock house. I think there's been a shooting."

"Jo Bailey?" Andy sounded scared. "I'm sorry. I'm sorry."

"Just get your butt to the rock house."

"I'm sorry, I'm sorry," he repeated, but I turned down the volume on the radio because I didn't want to listen to him whine.

I pulled the pry bar from behind my passenger seat and approached the front door again. The sound made as I pried the door open could have woken the dead. With a scream and a bang the latch popped free. I stepped in and shined my flashlight around. Mr. Bailey sat in his overstuffed chair, a book on his lap. My heart must have skipped a beat. The whole scene was deathly quite.

Mr. Bailey's head and shirt were soaked in blood. I hurried over to him worried that he might have been killed, and examined him with the flashlight. The side of his head was badly cut but seemed merely a flesh wound. His pulse was strong. The lantern had been hit by the other shot. I shined my flashlight around and located a second lantern. I took a moment to pump and light and was rewarded when the rock house became bathed in warm kerosene light.

I used canteen water and clean gauze from my red cross kit, to clean the wound. Mr. Bailey groaned and seemed to regain a weak consciousness.

"The wound will need stitches," I told him.

"My head hurts," Mr. Bailey said. "I have to lie down."

I helped Mr. Bailey to his bed. The inside of the rock house was one big room with his overstuffed chair and a small kitchen table with one chair at one end and the bed at the other. I covered him in case of shock. I put one of his monogramed towels under his head to keep blood off the pillow.

I used the next little while to look for slugs in the walls or elsewhere inside. I didn't find any in any of the mortar between the rocks or any sign of a ricochet off any of the rocks. Eventually lights lit the drive when Andy and the Lester arrived. I met them at the door.

"Andy," I said, with my official voice, and pointed at the rise opposite the outhouse. "Scour that direction for shell casings or anything else that might be helpful." Of course, that was the wrong direction, I learned later. I never would have expected the shooter to move to the other side of the house. The side without windows. That didn't compute.

"Evening Lester." I shook Lester's hand and noticed he still wore his leg support.

I led him to the bed. "A bullet grazed the side of Mr. Bailey's head."

Lester leaned over Mr. Bailey and examined him. "Need stitches."

I asked, "You want to do that?"

"No, I'll use compression bandages. I'll stitch him up tomorrow."

Mr. Bailey said, in a weak voice, "My head hurts."

"You have bad reactions to morphine?" Lester asked.

"None."

I put my hand on Lester's arm. "Let me question him first."

Lester nodded and went to the small kitchen table to prepare an injection.

I sat on the edge of the bed. "Mr. Bailey," I asked him. "Do you know you've been shot?"

"I figured so when the lantern exploded. I got up to find another light when a baseball bat hit me in the side of the head."

"Yeah. The holes in the window look like a large caliber, like from a hunting rifle. You know anyone around that might want to hurt you?"

He smiled that weird smile again, like he knew something I didn't. "Not from around these parts."

Andy clomped in through the front door. "Nothing much out there," he said. He held out his hand and displayed an assortment of shell casings. But they were all too old.

"Is that Jo Bailey?" Andy said, and walked up to Mr. Bailey, I guess so that he could brag to others about how he got so close to the famous man.

I was surprised and Andy appeared surprised too when Mr. Bailey reached up and grabbed his arm. "You'll be shot," he said to Andy. "But you won't die. You'll die in a car crash."

Doc returned with the syringe.

Mr. Bailey let go of Andy's hand.

Andy jumped back as if he had been stung. "What's that mean?" he asked. Bullet casings hit the floor as Andy dropped them.

Lester pushed Andy aside and sat next to Mr. Bailey. He found a vein and started to slowly inject the morphine.

"A big truck," Mr. Bailey said. He looked straight at Lester. "You won't see death approach. The truck will hit you and kill you instantly."

"That's old news," Lester said. "I don't drive anymore." He finished the injection and removed the needle.

"Is that the morphine talking?" I asked Lester.

Andy backed up to the front door. "What did he mean?"

"Doesn't act that fast," Lester said.

Mr. Bailey's eyes started to glaze over as the morphine took effect.

Andy backed slowly out the door without a glance backward and stood there and asked over and over, "What did he mean? What did he mean?"

About to tell Andy to get is butt back inside, when his body wiggled like a distorting lens or a reflection in water. Then he fell and I heard the shot. A high powered rifle shot that echoed off the hills around, but I couldn't detected its direction. I rushed to the door and called back to Lester, "Douse the light."

I waited inside the door for the light to go out. I drew my gun and flicked off the safety. Andy lay on his back with his legs at an odd angle. He opened his eyes and looked up at me. "Hurts," he said.

The light went out so I stepped outside and fired nine shots in the direction I figured the shot came from the direction past the outhouse.

Behind me I heard Lester say, "He's shot bad. I got to get him back to the clinic right away."

In the distance, a roar. "What's that?" I muttered. I refilled my clip while I listened. The roar increased and settled to a putt-putt. The sound was a that of diesel engine. A big one. I started to run. I ran up the low hill with nine fresh rounds in my gun. The engine sounded like a big truck ready to escape.

I got to the top of the hill but couldn't see anything. Then I caught the flash of a brake lights. The truck part of an eighteen-wheeler without the trailer started to move.

Behind me Andy's car started. I looked but the sound didn't compute. I couldn't figure out how Andy could drive if he'd been shot.

I tried to locate the truck again but without brake lights I couldn't pinpoint its location. Then the truck shifted gears and got closer. The truck roared into view. It sped along Cedar Canyon Road with lights off. It headed past us towards Barstow. I fired nine more shots, but figured I couldn't hit the side of a barn in the dark, moving that fast, and that far away.

Then headlights came on and Andy's car speed down the drive toward Cedar Canyon Road. The truck smashed into Andy's car broadside.

The truck hardly slowed. Once past the wrecked car the driver sped up again and turned on his headlights. The truck disappeared over the incline toward Mr. Aloshapman's place, but I was already running toward the wrecked car, screaming over and over "No! No! No!"

Damn you Mr. Bailey.

Lester and Andy were both killed in that wreck. As if you planned their death. But you couldn't have, could you? You were wounded yourself and unconscious with morphine.

But still. All those weeks and months. All those times we drove Lester ourselves, so he wouldn't have to drive himself. Since last summer. I mean why couldn't you have told him he would die in the winter?

I reported the truck to the Highway Patrol and the Arizona State Police but no sign of such a vehicle ever turned up. Of course, I didn't have a license number.

Andy's body was shipped to Goodland, Kansas, to his parents. Lester was buried next to his dad and mom in Riverview Cemetery out on West Broadway. His sister flew back from Paris for the funeral. A fine woman who seemed to take an immediate dislike to me. My dad introduced her around. She let my dad sell the property; her dad's house and the clinic. For one moment we were alone together and she told me, "I blame you for my brother's death." That was all. On that same evening she flew back to Paris.

A lot of people asked me if the brace on his leg caused him to die. I always said the same thing, "A truck hit the car. A brace on his leg made no difference."

A week after Lester was buried I got another call from Mr. Aloshapmen.

"A big truck drove by a little while ago. Sorta like a moving truck. Then that odd jeep from the rock house followed a little while later. I was curious, so I checked out the rock house. And Sheriff?"

"Yes, Mr. Aloshapmen."

"The rock house is empty. Nothing is there. All the windows are gone. The roof is gone. The outhouse is gone. Like nobody was ever there. Just gone, poof."

I felt a chill run up my back. "Thanks," I said. "I'll send Andy to check. . . ," then I caught myself for the umteenth time. "I mean I'll be out to check myself soon."

I never did check on the rock house. Officers came out from the county seat to investigate. I figure they asked Mr. Bailey lots of question. And I bet you some of them didn't like the answers they got. I can bet you that with certainty.

Lester was hit by a truck like Mr. Bailey said. I finally read Mr. Bailey's books and discovered that he didn't know too. Mr. Bailey learned early that he couldn't save anyone that was going to die. He learned that lesson, but he clearly didn't realize that other people, hadn't learned that lesson yet. We struggled and hoped and pretended we'd licked death, and then we were proved wrong. And I hurt. I mean I hurt bad.

Of course the story didn't end there. Nothing ever ends clean like that.

Mrs. Dodson, owner of the Bar-X ranch, was in town and spotted me inside Juicy's restaurant. She tapped on the glass and indicated she'd like to join me.

I nodded and smiled.

"I'm Mrs. Dodson," she said and sat. "Too bad about the doctor and your deputy,"

"Yeah, too bad."

"What will you do?"

"The county will send somebody else out to be deputy. Any day soon, I suppose."

Mrs. Dodson opened her purse. She was younger than I thought, perhaps in her mid thirties. She was well dressed in expensive linen cut in a cowboy style. She pulled out a check. "After Jo Bailey moved out, after he was shot." She slid the check forward face up. "Got this check in the mail. Course I don't need money and I figure his signature might be worth more some day."

I looked at the check. Made out for a quarter million dollars, and signed by Jo Bailey.

I grinned, I'm not sure why. Irony perhaps. "Yeah. You may be right. That check might be worth a lot some day."

"I bet so." Mrs. Dodson picked up the check. "Jo Bailey has disappeared again."

"That so?"

"Got himself kidnapped." Mrs. Dodson dropped the check back in her purse.

"That so?"

"Too bad Doc Wilson, the son, got killed because Jo Bailey said so."

I sat up straight. "No, Lester didn't die because Mr. Bailey said so. He was hit by a truck, and Mr. Bailey foresaw his death. He predicted, he didn't cause anything."

"Are you sure?"

"Positive."

Mrs. Dodson stood. "Jo Bailey ever tell how you would eventually to die?"

I had to think about that. "Maybe," I told her. "Something about a chicken with its foot caught in the crack of a table."

Mrs. Dodson looked at me as I had said something that made no sense at all. "Well you take care Sheriff," she said at last. "I mean Wayne. Mr. Wayne

Manley. But you think about what I said. Cause and effect. Sometimes, well they're not that easy to see."

I half stood to be polite. Mrs. Dodson walked outside and back to her car. "Made death happen, hah!" I said, and sat down again. "I swear some people believe the dumbest things."

And they do you know. Over the years there's been all sorts of stories about how Mr. Bailey predicted death. I even found out he predicted his own death. Isn't that a kick in the pants. And there was nothing he could do. Even though he predicted his own death, he couldn't prevent himself from death in the end.

My dad died a few years ago. He'd been in the hospital after a minor stroke and, well, he died a little while later. I was a surprised. One day he was alive with plans to go home and then next day he wasn't and I didn't see his death coming.

So you see that's not why I'm so pissed at Mr. Bailey. Not because he predicted Lester's death. I'm angry with him because left me thinking I could prevent that death. He left me with hope. Then he snatched my hope away. So no. No thank you.

Part 3

The Final Years

Events Of 1982
Dahlia Phillips

Her journal written prior to her suicide

Saturday, January 3, 1982

I woke up with a hose run up my nose and down my throat. It burned and felt awful. But how did I feel about the experience? That's what I'm supposed to do. Write about what happened to me and how I got inside, and what I feel. That sucks, but what I really feel. I mean shit!

They told me the police found me not breathing. I lay on a sidewalk with a fifth of vodka, mostly empty, and an empty bottle of barbiturates on the ground next to me. I bet the booze was Gordon's, that's the cheap crap I drank mostly back then. Then they pumped my stomach. I woke up with the black rubber hose up my nose and a doctor told me this might hurt and then he pulled the tube out, and crap that hose smelled bad on the way out and hurt and stung for a long time after.

I'm locked up in a nut house for people who tried to kill themselves. I didn't try to kill myself. That's what I try to tell them but they hear what they want to hear and don't listen to me. I got drunk and took pills and I didn't see the connection. Dumb, sure, but I didn't try to kill myself.

My good grey pants, the ones I made from a pattern I bought at Woolworths, were ripped along the left side when I fell. They won't give me a needle or thread to fix them so I have to walk around in torn pants. Makes me look and feel like a bum, a lopsided bum. Good thing I don't limp!

Bryan Costales

Sunday the 4th

The people in lockup with me are the really crazy ones, not me. I sit with my feet pulled up on a chair because the floor was washed last night and I can still smell the ammonia. One of the men walks slowly around all day in black slippers that have no back and flip and flop on the floor. He doesn't say anything to anybody. He's really tall, like a big old bird in a white, sleeveless t-shirt and striped flannel pajama pants, and a big hooked nose. Hold on! The woman in the chair next to me farted. I have to move. I'm on the couch, the one covered with sticky plastic. Anyway that man walks and walks mostly with his eyes closed. He never seems to bump into anything though, so there must be radar or something at work up there behind those closed eyes. I smell breakfast.

Last night a crazy woman named skinny Wendy crawled into bed with me. She got under the covers and shoved me to one side with her bony elbows. Gimme room, she said in her scratchy voice. Then she started to snore. Her BO was really rank. She didn't say anything mean or sexy. She crawled in, poked me away, and slept. I got up after she started to snore good and got one of the nurses to send her back to her own bed. But the nurse asked, why don't you trade beds? That seemed okay with me so I did.

When I woke up I was in her bed and skinny Wendy was in mine, at opposite ends of the women's sleep room. That must have been what skinny Wendy wanted in the first place because we slept in switched beds for the rest of the time I was in there. Other than that I never had any trouble with her.

How do I feel about that? Relieved, I guess, and glad. Sure, sometimes I lose weight, but I never get that skinny. She looks a real fright, like a skeleton with skin. And those bony elbows. I mean shit!

148

<u>Monday January 5</u>

The doctor gave me a list of questions to answer. Not a quiz, but more like who in your family or friends can you say anything to? I wrote down Nobody for most. True. Mom and dad and sister Alice all burned in that fire. The one that burned down the Santa Barbara mountains a few years back. I lived with David at the time, in L.A. and didn't know that my parents decided to stay home, and to keep Alice home, and water down the roof with a garden hose. Stupid, stupid. They should have left. Why didn't they leave? Alice was only ten. I got nobody, even our dog Runner died in that fire.

None of my old boyfriends would do of course. I mean who can say anything at all to a boyfriend? Bite your tongue all the time. Say the wrong thing and he'll dump you.

The doctor didn't like my answers. He leaned on a pad of paper and looked at me with his eyes. He said I need someone that I can talk to anytime about anything. I told him to suggest someone. He scratched his bald head and told me that would probably be my outside therapist. Well if so, I say great. But we'll see.

<u>More Monday again</u>

A doctor I didn't know asked me a bunch of questions. He sat across from me in a plain wooden chair the same as mine, his hands folded on his lap. I told him I liked his suit. A pin-striped shiny fabric, probably wool or a silk mix. He asked me a question, and then asked over and over and finally I guess I couldn't take much more so I started to answer.

He wanted to know why I tried to kill myself. I said, I didn't. He asked about lovers and money and sex and booze and food. Then he asked about nightmares and that was something I wanted to talk about. I didn't tell him about my new nightmares, instead I told him about the old ones from before. The ones about huge black shadow heads, men's heads with large red hot mouths sewn shut with chains, but open anyway, and showed teeth and tried to gobble me into their fire filled mouths. I won't tell you more, because I hurt to remember those dreams. But the doc thought my dream was important. At the end he said he wouldn't see me again. He was a special doctor that only came in once a month. Lucky me. Good riddance I say.

Tuesday the 6th

My regular doctor, the bald one, wanted me to show him what I meant by everyone else is crazy. I walked out of his office with him and waited. The room was big with a high ceiling like a basket ball court, but with small painted white windows. Plain black wooden chairs and tables were scattered around the room. At the end near the locked door out, chairs were set in a circle but nobody sat. Finally the doctor said, Go ahead, show me. So I shifted my weight from one foot to the other because the floor was hard, and pointed

The first crazy person I pointed to was the tall man called Walter. He had foreign face, maybe Indian, with black hair and really dark brown, creepy eyes. He'd walk around naked all day, dressed in only a thin cotton blanket that he said was his super cape. If you stopped and asked him anything, he'd finger his limp cock and say, I'll save you. Weird and crazy. Save me from what?

Then there was Julie, the Humpty Dumpty woman. Her arms and legs were normal, but her body was round and egg shaped. Not like she was fat, more like she was born that way. She would listen for the pay phone to ring and run to pick up. But she would pull off her top on her way to the phone, you know show off her small boobs, and put her clothes back on after she was done. But she wasn't too bright. She would listen to the person on the phone say something like, is Alice there? then would drop the phone and walk away and mutter, there's nobody. Usually the nurse came to rescue and saved most phone calls.

The old man with the long white beard sat in the same chair all the time by the window. The window were painted white so we couldn't see outside, but he sat there anyway leaned against the glass and recited lines from commercials. Like, I'm a pepper you're a pepper, and plop-plop fizz-fizz. But mostly he said, Tuesday is Red's Tamale Day over and over like a stuck record. But said those things sad-like and soft so I had to stand right behind him to hear him. He wore a dark green wool coat that looked rough and uncomfortable up close. I would listen to him and he didn't seem to know I was there. Like he tried to remember something, or maybe remember anything.

Then there was Moon. I don't know her real name, but she had a round pale, clown-white face like a full moon so I called her Moon. She would jog in circles around the room in long flowing pants under a too-big t-shirt. She looked hard all the time all around like she searched for someone. Then, every once in a while she dropped into one of the black wooden chairs by the back wall, her long legs wide, and talked to someone who wasn't there. While she talked, her face turned red like she argued with someone. But she was never loud, no not loud, but looked angry all the time.

The doctor said, yes, those people are crazy. But because they're crazy doesn't mean I'm sane. That didn't help at all, of course. I didn't feel crazy, but I guess I did try to kill myself. So what the heck.

Events Of 1994
Ace Hoklins

Father Bob Hoklins, The Church of Jo, Los Angeles, California

At eighteen I dropped out of high school and signed up for the army. I was bad-conduct discharged from boot camp because I stole small weapons and sold them to Mexican and Russian gangs. I drifted for a few years until my mid-twenties when I realized I had flushed my life down a toilet. About the only thing that kept me sane was my love of games and puzzles. I could wait for hours to get food stamps provided I had a crossword puzzle to work. And I could always find a newspaper discarded somewhere with a puzzle unsolved.

Like all young men, I sought something I could belong to. The army didn't work out and nearly landed me in jail. I tried to work for bookmaker in Las Vegas but found that work tedious and the hours awful. They taught me to count cards and that gave me a little extra income until the casinos blackballed me. I think what finally drove me out of Las Vegas was a cough I developed from the constant atmosphere of smoke and deception. There, under the tutelage of criminals, I legally changed my name to Ace Hoklins so that I could appear and act tougher.

Armed with a new ID, I left Nevada in search of fortune. But high paid work evaded me because of my work history and dishonorable discharge, until I eventually landed a job as a gardener at the big Presbyterian Church in Gilroy. The front resembled a rocket about to takeoff, an astute symbol I felt for an institute of worship. The work was honest but unsettled in a way. I liked to work in soil and to be surrounded by greenery and colorful flowers. Growth and rebirth and all that, but this job appeared dead-end, another with no future.

The Presbyterian priest was a young man like myself, perhaps a few years older. His name was Father Desmond and he liked to bounce ideas off me. I stood in the garden and leaned on a shovel under a warm California afternoon sky and listen to his mellow voice.

"Hoklins," he might say, "Man cannot know the future, only God knows what is to come. But because of our free-will we can change the future based on our choices. Does our free-will, our choice, limit God's ability to know?"

I don't think he actually sought my opinion. Rather he posed questions like puzzles to me, to cause me to think about God and free-will and morality. His process was gradual and spanned half a year, and wore me down like a rock rolled smooth by the current of a constant river.

Eventually I opened up to him and revealed that I never had a father. My mother never mentioned the mysterious man who was my father, not even on her death bed. Instead I had been raised by a long series of week- to month-long dads who dated my mom. Some good, most bad. I also told Father Desmond about my bad-conduct discharge and the years I worked in gambling. He understood but remained compassionate. He told me about an organization a short way up 101 in Morgan Hill. The place was, he told me, a loose collection of not-so-honorably discharged men who worked together to help themselves. He offered to drive me up there and did so on the next Monday.

Events of 1987-1998
Dustin Willowsmith

Reporter for the San Francisco Examiner, Reconstructed notes of several stories about Jo Bailey

My tale about Jo Bailey began while I researched
a piece about missing children in the Bay area. I happened upon an AP feed story about an FBI bust in the
foothills of Northern California. The story mentioned Jo
Bailey and that he had been kidnapped and later found
and freed. I knew that Jo Bailey lived in San Francisco,
so I took the story to my Editor, Greg Brady, and
argued that story might be worth a follow-up.

Greg was an old-school editor and would never
agree to a story unless a real chance existed that it
might hit the front page. Myopic in his thick glasses, he
could see through my attempt to sidestep his authority. "Jo Bailey's old news," he said. "So he was kidnapped," he shrugged. "That's hardly news."

"I'm still working on that piece you wanted about
the ballooning housing market. I thought maybe Jo
Bailey's mansion might make an amusing contrast."

Greg agreed with an absent minded wave of his
manicured hand.

I drove out to Jo Bailey's mansion in the Seacliff
neighborhood of San Francisco, where I hoped to interview him.

The Seacliff neighborhood lay at the northwest-
ern edge of the city. It overlooked the Pacific Ocean and
the Golden Gate Bridge. An exclusive area that was
home to the filthy or old rich. I drove up a road that
was lined with beautifully trimmed gardens and bor-

dered by spotless sidewalks. Jo Bailey's house was at the corner turn before Lake Street.

I pulled into his wide driveway and discovered a real-estate salesman parked there who leaned against his white BMW convertible. I introduced myself

"Bob Kirby with Sepal and Mason Realty, he said.

"Jo Bailey's place?" I asked.

Mr. Kirby was a bit too formally dressed for warm weather. A pale blue sport coat and fancy gold dive-watch told me he had a bit of discretional money. His tie was plaid but subdued, definitely not a power tie. I shook his hand and his grip was firm and friendly.

"Was," Mr. Kirby said. He pulled a flier from a thin briefcase that was open on the hood of his car and handed me one. "He moved out last week."

I noticed the sales price and whistled. "Any idea where he went?"

"None. All proceeds from the sale go to a list of charities." He rifled through his briefcase again. "Yes," he said, and handed me a sheet of paper. "A copy of the list." Then he said, "Hey, you want to see the place?"

"You bet," I said.

I expected the inside to be a classic mansion. You know, art everywhere and expensive furniture spread over expensive carpets. But once inside, I was startled by how stark the place appeared.

Just behind the front wooden doors was a second set of thick, steel doors that stood swung-open inward. They appeared to work with hydraulics and to interlock in some impenetrable way. I raised my eyebrows, but Mr. Kirby shrugged and nodded at the stairway ahead.

Beyond the steel doors a gated stairway ran straight up to a second floor landing. The sides of the stairway were wrapped in steel bars all the way up. White closed circuit cameras hung high in every corner.

"Is this a house or a fort?" I asked Mr. Kirby.

"Both," he said. "The walls are three foot thick concrete. You have to go up those stairs and down again to enter the living area. I'll show you."

As we walked up the stairs I noticed rifle slots that were only visible once on the stairs and trapped there by the enclosed bars. We reached the top and I faced yet another door, a bank's safe door, but thinner and rectangular. The door was open and sunlight shined up through from below.

I paused there and looked back down the barred stairs. "Was he ever attacked?"

"No," Mr. Kirby said. "I asked him that myself and he laughed." Mr. Kirby leaned conspiratorially in, close enough so I could smell his sandalwood after-shave. "He went for a walk, in disguise of course, a blond wig, sun glasses, and gay clothes. But his body-guard had to come back inside for something, a PDA or cellphone, I imagine. That's when they nabbed him. While he waited right outside his front door."

I glanced back down the stairs again. "You mean right out front of his fortress?"

Mr. Kirby laughed. "Yeah. I guess that's why his place is for sale."

I shook my head at the irony of his kidnapping.

Mr. Kirby gestured at the door that lead to down the other side. "Want to see the real house?"

On the other side was another stairway down, covered in lush carpet and bordered with a delicate wooden banister. The room below looked like the man-sions I'd seen before. Art, a piano, and fine furniture tastefully arranged. On a small table near the bottom of the stairs was a pile of brochures and a chilled bucket wish a champagne bottle and a tray of hors d'oeuvres. I tasted a Russian Osetra caviar-stuffed mushroom and complemented Mr. Kirby on the quality.

"Everything personal had been removed," Mr. Kirby said, with a wave of his hand. "The art and furniture have been rented to aid in the sale. There's nothing really left of Jo Bailey's. Nothing he actually owned by him other than the house, that is."

I sensed my story drift away from under me. "No idea where he went?"

"Just those charities," he nodded at the folded paper I still held in my hand.

I thanked him and wandered the mansion. I couldn't see how Jo Bailey's home could fit into a story about ballooning house prices. I sipped champagne from a thin glass and marveled at the Olympic sized pool on the lower level. Blue light rippled across a low white-marble ceiling in a room that smelled fresh, not of chlorine. "What next?" I asked myself. I made a mental note then to send a thank you to Mr. Kirby.

Back at work the next day, I phoned all the charities that were on the list Mr. Kirby had given me. None of the ones I called knew where Jo Bailey had gone. But one, who insisted he remain anonymous, provided an important clue.

The voice on the other end of the telephone had an odd accent I couldn't place. "The grant of funds is bonded," the voice said. "The only odd thing is that the bonding company is in the Philippines."

"Where in the Philippines?"

"Doesn't say. We have a phone number."

The person on the phone gave me the number and made me promise not to print or otherwise reveal that number. Just to be safe, I didn't write that number in my notes.

That evening I figured the next business day had finally begun in the Philippines. I had fixed myself a tomato basil and mozzarella salad with a glass of a nice Napa pinot noir. Satiated, I sat at my Mac in what I jokingly call my home office and called the number I'd been given.

"Mr. D'Trang," the voice on the phone said. "Transaction Bonding, Ltd. How may I help you?"

I identified myself and asked, "Are you able to get in touch with Jo Bailey."

The man on the phone hesitated. "Yes."

"Do you have his address?"

"No."

"Do you have a phone number for him?"

"Yes."

"Can you give the number to me?"

"No."

"Is that a local number there in Manila?"

"Yes,"

At the other end the phone's mouthpiece was covered which muffled conversation.

The man on the phone cleared his throat and said, "Sorry. I'll have to hang up."

"Well thanks for talking to me."

"Good bye," he said.

I tried to reason out what must have happened to Jo Bailey. He must have thought he would be safer in the Philippines, so he moved there. Odd choice, I thought. I poured myself a second glass of that good pinot noir and dialed a friend of mine in Manila. He was a reporter there that I had known from my UCLA days. I asked him to find Jo Bailey for me.

A week later my friend called back. The phone rang as I returned to my apartment. I dropped my bag by the front door and grabbed the hallway phone.

"No luck." my friend said. "Just rumors. Some say he is in the north. Some say he lives under a new name somewhere in Manila. But rumors, that's all."

I thanked him and the next day wrote my story, a short piece than ran on page three. Basically that Jo Bailey was believed to have gone into hiding in the Philippines.

A week or so passed without event. One afternoon, Greg my editor leaned over my desk and joked, "Jo Bailey still missing?"

I smiled and ignored him, but his comment piqued my curiosity again. That afternoon I telephoned the publisher of Jo Bailey's second book.

"I'm Dustin Willowsmith with the Examiner newspaper in San Francisco. I want to track down Jo Bailey for an interview."

"Good luck," the woman on the phone laughed. "We've tried to find him for two months."

"You mean for taxes?"

"No. We need his go-ahead to print his third book."

"What's the title?"

"The 3rd Book of Jo, what else?"

"Any chance I can get a copy to review?"

"None. But give me your address. If he ever gives us the go, I will send you a copy."

I gave her my address and hung up.

I ran out of ideas. The only solution I could think of was to ask my editor to pay for a private eye. Toward that end I invited him to lunch with me at the Blue Butterfly, that new high-end restaurant out on the Embarcadero.

Greg looked around at the swagged fabrics and profusion of fresh flowers and asked, "A gay restaurant?"

I noted the pinks and lavenders and momentarily wondered the same thing myself. But I knew the chef personally so merely said, "Nope. Not that I know of."

Greg whistled a soft low whistle when he read the menu. He looked at me over the top of that tall thin document. "I didn't know I paid you enough to eat at such a place."

I chuckled and we engaged in small-talk until our drinks came then I toasted, my screwdriver clinked his Courvoisier in a heated snifter. I launched right into my request, "Look Greg. Something's up with Jo Bailey. I feel certain, in my bones. But I need the paper to help me hire a private investigator. You think I could talk you into that?"

Greg mock choked on his drink. "You crazy?" he told me. "The story's dead. If Jo Bailey ever comes back, that will be a story. If Bobby Fisher ever comes back, that will be a story. See me when one or the other happens."

Events Of 1982
Dahlia Phillips

Her journal written prior to her suicide

Tuesday, January 13, 1982

I'm home! The doctors gave me a drug that made me want to sit and watch TV all day. I couldn't read or write while I took that stuff. Those pills weren't like the pot I smoked before, even the strong stuff. They didn't make me hungry, only kinda stoned. I had to take them until I got out. The doctor told me I really had to keep up my journal. I would see a different doctor when I got out, and the new journal stuff would help. So instead I'll write about my home.

I couldn't believe my apartment when I got home. I opened the door and right away smelled the garbage gone bad. I had to hold my nose and carry the bag out to the big dumpster out back. Then I opened the fridge and the same thing. Half or more of my food had gone bad and smelled really bad too. I threw out some hamburger meat that had cost me a bundle.

I took a shower in my own bath and that felt good. Good to be home even though I could only afford a tiny apartment. The soap smelled right, not like the soap in the looney bin. And my towels are soft and green, not white and hard. I got dressed again in clean clothes. I pulled out the sewing machine and fixed my good pants, not perfect of course, but good enough. After that I sat and actually felt human again, or as human as I have in a long time. Human, yes.

Another Tuesday February 3

I got a new doctor yesterday and he was pissed I stopped writing in my journal. He made me promise I would write something at least once a week. He said, pick a day and make that day a habit. I picked Tuesdays because of that crazy old guy in the loony bin. The guy with the long white beard who said over and over, Tuesday is Red's Tamale Day. He never said what that meant, but I like tamales and his words stuck in my head and made me think that Tuesday is the day to write.

I was glad my welfare checks still showed up. I guess the welfare people never talked to the doctors. One check to the landlord, food stamps for food, another check for utilities, and a tiny bit left over for me. I always cashed the checks at the corner store. The Chinese man behind the counter knew me and would let me buy anything with my food stamps even though he wasn't supposed to. But I had to see him, his wife never let me do that. She never smiled at me either.

Tuesday the 10th

I woke up with an empty bottle of vodka on my pillow. I wanted more but I was broke until the next check. The doctor was really pissed I missed my appointment. I didn't tell him I was drunk, I told him I was sick.

Tuesday the 17th

Damn, damn, damn. I shouldn't have written I was drunk in my journal. The doctor told me I was an alcoholic. I told him no I wasn't. He said, then why did I lie? Stupid, stupid, stupid.

Saturday May 1 and the freak rain ended.

I stopped writing because I got a new doctor who didn't care if I wrote. I found a journal in my underwear drawer and read the whole thing. Boy was I ever a sicko back then. Not any more. I went to AA meetings and I've been dry for over two months. I wish I had money for clothes because they're all too big. Some I can take in, but some look stupid after I take them in, don't hang right anymore or pucker when I walk. Good thing I have belts.

The reason I write this is because I met a cousin of mine, a cousin I didn't know I had. I don't know how he found me, but he did, and I felt good to meet with him. He's about as close to a family as I have anymore.

He works for the government and travels a lot. He told me what he did but that didn't make any sense to me. He said over and over that family was important and that I should call him if I ever needed help. He gave me a phone number that he said was good forever.

His name was Bob Whallen, and his mother was my mother's sister. His mom was dead too, cancer he told me. He wasn't married and didn't have any kids so his family was gone too. He asked me what I did and I told him I was on welfare. He said, when he got back from Uganda he would see me again and help me get a job. I said, that was okay with me.

Bob made me think about family. I wondered what ever happened to my daughter Joy. I gave her away when she was born. I wonder all the time, I she okay? Does she work in a good job? Maybe married to a good man with a family of her own? Did she ever get the letter I sent care of the hospital? I hope she's never stuck in a loony bin like I was.

Tuesday! June, I think, the 1st

Red's Tamale Day! I gave my welfare check to the landlord and he gave me change in dollar bills. Then I tried to find a cheap tamale. Found one on Figueroa street in that little restaurant behind the closed Goodwill store. Man that tamale was delicious.

When I got home there was a note pinned to my door. The note was from Jo Bailey, an old, old boyfriend of mine and the father of Joy. He invited me to an art opening. I've never been to an art opening. I walked by them before of course on the sidewalk. All dressed up people inside looked at art. I always notice that they give out free drinks and snacks. Art openings, because of the free snacks mostly, maybe I should meet him.

Events Of 1994
Ace Hoklins

Father Bob Hoklins, The Church of Jo, Los Angeles,
California

The organization was housed in a concrete slab warehouse slung low by the railroad tracks. A long line of silver garage-style rollup doors and black normal-sized doors alternated into the near distance. The man who ran the program stepped from a middle warehouse door that was rolled up all the way open. He had deep black eyes, a full head of black hair and a gray trimmed beard. He smiled and his teeth needed work. We shook hands and he introduced himself as Defoe Scallody. "I run everything," he told me. "You can stay and sleep on one of the cots in the back room, or you can visit when you have a ride. Those that don't stay drift away." He poked me with a finger. "You're not a drifter are you?"

DeFoe seemed iffy and I was tempted to turn and walk away. But a few of the other guys wandered out then and they seemed okay. One introduced himself as George Wriggles, administratively discharged from the Marines. "My specialty," he said. "I made and defused bombs."

"That must have been frightening," I said.

"I still have nightmares. But Mr. Scallody has helped. I don't have nearly as many bad dreams anymore." He smiled at Mr. Scallody

Mr. Scallody looked me over. "What did you do that got you discharged?"

"Sold small arms to gangs, mostly."

Mr. Scallody put his hand on my shoulder. "You'll do," he said. I noticed his breath smelled like garlic.

"You eat a lot of garlic?" I asked him.

"Lots." He patted his chest. "Keeps a man strong."

I told Father Desmond I'll stay.

He said, "I'd be pleased to welcome you back any time you need to return to your job." He smiled. "As gardener."

I shook his hand and watched him drive away in his old beat-up Volvo. I was sad to see him go. Even though young, he had been more like a dad to me than any dad or step dad I had ever known.

At first I thought that Defoe Scallody was a psychologist or therapist of some kind. He would hold group sessions. The seven of us sat round in a circle and he would help us bring our guilts and fears to the surface. He had a direct way about him that slowly earned my respect. I didn't suspect, then, that he was a murderer. I thought he was odd, but didn't suspect he could be dangerous.

There was a newspaper rack at the end of the block. I would pick up an L.A. Times there every morning and would work all the puzzles. I got to know the Datworthy brothers because they liked to solve anagrams. Evan was into computers and electronics. He was less easy for me to talk to because he talked mostly about technical things. His brother Sam was older than Evan and a foot taller. He was a body guard by trade but gentle with the guys. In addition to anagrams, he liked to find the differences in the two pictures in the Sunday paper.

After a month and a half, I got to know everyone. One day Defoe Scallody called me into his cramped office. He asked me if I trusted him, and I answered, "Sure. Why not?"

"You've helped us for six weeks, so I finally I have a job for you," he said. He waited for me to say something. I could think of nothing to say, so he continued. "I need you to pick me up a high powered sniper's rifle with ammo that can't be traced. You can do that can't you?"

I nodded, puzzled by the request.

Defoe smiled. "How much?"

"Depends on how high a quality you want. Anywhere, say from $500 to $5000 and up."

He smiled with those bad teeth and opened his desk drawer and pulled out a thick manila envelope. "Should do." he said, and handed me the envelope; sealed but seriously heavy with money.

Well, I got a ride with another of the men, Larry Yonkers who was the only guy with a car. While on the drive I quizzed Larry. "Why does Mr. Scallody need gun?"

Larry prided himself on how many cars and trucks he knew how to drive. He habitual pushed his long black hair out of his eyes as he drove which made me grip the arm rest firmly. Larry tended to answer questions with questions, "You ever hear of Jo Bailey?"

"No. Why?"

"Hasn't Mr. Scallody told you yet?" he asked and refused to discuss the matter anymore that trip.

I found an excellent Remington 700 Police Model in Fresno. I spent less than I expected which pleased me. I asked Larry to stop by a bookstore so I could buy a book of puzzles. He didn't mind and waited in the car so I snuck a look for anything about Jo Bailey. I was surprised to find he'd written two books. I thumbed through them and didn't find anything of interest, a lot of religious mumo jumbo. I returned to the car with a book of Merl Reagle crossword puzzles.

We return to the warehouse earlier than I expected, perhaps a testament to Larry's driving. I handed the rifle and change to Mr. Scallody who expertly disassembled and laid the pieces on his desk. I could see he was experienced with rifles. He thanked me and I turned to leave.

But I hesitated then turned back and asked, "Who is Jo Bailey?"

"Who told you that?"

"I overheard the guys talk."

He dropped the envelope into his desk drawer, slid that drawer closed. "Come with me," he said, and led me out of the office. He locked the office then took me outside and down the row of rollup doors to the last one at the end. He took a key from a chain around his neck and opened the door next to the rollup door in that last warehouse.

Inside was a large room the walls of which were filled with photographs and newspaper articles. From the middle of the room they resembled a crossword puzzle perhaps designed under LSD or a collage designed by a mad artist. I walked up to the nearest wall and looked. All the individual pieces of paper appeared to be about someone name Jo Bailey. I looked at Mr. Scallody. "Him?"

Mr. Scallody smiled and waved his hand toward a seat. In the center of the office, two overstuffed old brown leather chairs faced each other separated by a few feet. Each had a an identical small table. I sat in the one indicated furthest from the door. Mr. Scallody handed me a cold can of beer from a refrigerator I hadn't noticed. He sat in the other chair. In that moment I felt we were about to face off over a game of chess but without a chessboard.

"Jo Bailey is the personification of evil," Mr. Scallody said. "Remember that. But first I'll tell you a little story."

He leaned back and arched his fingers. "When Jo Bailey was a kid, he predicted my dad would hang himself. But what really happened is Jo's father and mother came over and hung my dad, murdered him. They made up evidence to suggest a suicide. When I came home and found him, I realized at once the note he left was not in my dad's hand writing."

He paused and gazed at me. I got the impression he wanted to measure me up. He waited for the correct reaction. I didn't mention that I had seen Jo Bailey's books in the bookstore. I suspected I shouldn't have done any research on my own.

"I was eighteen," he continued. "I turned the house upside down but couldn't find my dad's pistol anywhere. They'd stolen that too. I tried to tell the police but they didn't believe me. Why would a middle class couple murder anyone they asked me. I tried to explain, but they laughed."

"You ever find the gun?" I asked.

"No, but wait. The next thing Jo predicted was the death of his mother. He predicted that she would be shot by a stranger. But I found out he left school early that day. Found out from a school chum of his. What I figure is Jo snuck into his own house and killed his own mother with my gun."

"Ah," I said, because I couldn't think of anything else to say.

"The cops questioned me because the killer used my dad's gun, but why would I want to kill his mother? I mean, they said, my dad's death was a suicide." He shrugged. "Where was my motive?"

He stood then and gestured at the walls. "I've followed Jo Bailey all these years and have collected lots of evidence that he is a charlatan and a con artist." He began to pace. "I've documented dozens of times he predicted a death and then either carried out the murder himself or hired someone to kill for him. Look," He pointed at a newspaper article, "He predicted a man would be blown off a roof. Later the man had fallen off his home roof and struck his head wrong and died. And look," he pointed at a copy of a hotel bill. "Jo Bailey happened to stay at a hotel in that same town on that same day and never before or after."

"Circumstantial," I muttered, unsure what I should say.

"Exactly!" He snapped his fingers and gestured with his index finger. "But when you see the same pattern over and over, everything starts to add up to, well, to murder."

"Have you shown me everything?"

He walked behind my chair and put his hand on my shoulder. "Ace," he said. "There's seven of us counting you. And our mission is to kill Jo Bailey. Our mission is to kill the killer of my dad. Our mission is to kill a murderer who has gotten away with murder too long."

I felt uncomfortable with his hand still on my shoulder but didn't dare shrug it off. "That seems easy," I said. "I mean he's merely a man, right?"

He removed his hand and walked around to stand in front of me again. He said, "Maybe." He sat down. "And maybe not." He leaned back and rubbed his beard thoughtfully. "You see I tried once already. I shot at him from the audience when he gave a speech at the Greek Theater in Berkeley. I missed but killed someone else by accident. I got 20 years for that. I was paroled after 12 years and have only been out six years so far. You see," he leaned forward. "I have to play my hand close to the vest for the next couple years, because of the parole."

"You only try that once?"

He looked away from me like he was embarrassed or ashamed. "I found out once that he had a string of post office boxes spread over the state. I figure he had to check them every once in a while." He looked at me again. "Rain fell in buckets that night and darkness shrouded the post office. So, what the hell," he shrugged. "I shot the wrong man. He was a hired hand of Jo Bailey's sent to pick up the mail."

I watched him carefully. "I see what you mean," I said. "By he's hard to kill."

That's why I need good men like yourself. To do jobs that I can't do myself."

"Like what?"

"Like the reason you got me that rifle. I have another chance to kill him. Out in the Mojave Desert. A chance to put an end Jo the monster once and for all."

I finished the beer. I wasn't sure what I should say so I belched to buy time. "I'm not a killer," I said at last.

"I know," he seemed relieved. "You'll be in a support role."

He walked over and held out his hand. I stood and shook his hand. He said, "Welcome aboard."

Events of 1987-1998
Dustin Willowsmith

Reporter for the San Francisco Examiner, Reconstructed notes of several stories about Jo Bailey

Christmas and New Years arrived and fled and then Greg wandered past my desk again and said, "Did you see that Bobby Fisher died?"

He had a smug look on his face. I said, "I notice you weren't invited to the funeral." Actually nobody from outside Island was invited, so Greg laughed and walked away.

Some four or so months passed, then a page proof copy of Jo Bailey's third book arrived in the mail. I took the next weekend off and read the entire manuscript.

I understand why Jo Bailey has gone into hiding. In his third book, he claimed to have inhabited the next-dimension lives of such dignitaries as the last Buddha, Mohammed, and Joseph Smith. He spent an entire chapter on each and used each as proof that God could not exist.

He also explained how explosive death of the brain prevented memories from survival into next dimension. His reasons seemed weak to me, but I can see how that point of view might anger some.

My editor didn't feel that publication of his book was newsworthy. He said, "Give the book to Jim Abrams to review. A book's not really news." Jim Abrams was our book reviewer.

I telephoned Jo's book editor again.

"Are you sure you want to publish his book. Aren't you at risk."

"That's what I thought too. But I was told not to worry. Evidently, Jo Bailey took out one hundred million dollars in insurance to indemnify us."

I whistled.

"Yeah. And we also set up a dummy company to do the actual publication. Naturally all this is on the QT. You can't reveal anything."

I promised and said, "I look forward to the storm his book may create."

"Me too. Yes, me too."

A month later the book was published. Because I had already read the book,. I was prepared for the fire storm of criticism that followed.

I was set to drop Jo Bailey from my list projects when a note arrived from his publisher.

"Dear Mr. Willowsmith," the note began. "We received the enclosed letter from a woman who claims to be Jo Bailey's daughter. Because she is in a psychiatric institute in Chicago, we lack the resources to follow up. Therefore we pass the letter to you, a reporter, who likely has the resources."

The enclosed letter was from a Joy Hope Luxlishski:

> My mother is Dallia Phillips. She got word
> to me before she died that my real father is
> Jo Bailey. I have no claim on anything that
> is his, his royalties or anything else. I
> simply want to find him and speak to him.
> Please help me if you are able.

My paper reduced its staff before I could contact Joy Luxlishski, and I was let go from my reporter job. Her brief letter was considered newspaper property so I could not take her letter with me.

Fortunately these notes were at home. I contacted a lawyer I knew who performed pro-bono work for needy people. I sent a transcribed copy of Joy's letter to him and asked him to let me know how things turned out.

In the meanwhile I needed another job but not right away because I had enough savings to hold me for a few months. I made some calls and landed a food reviewer job at the LA Times. Not the head food reviewer, mind you, but one of several on a staff of junior (also known as low paid) reviewers.

At my new job, I stumbled across the following curious Los Angeles Times anonymous letter to the editor:

> A new church, only in existence for two
> years, The Church of Jo, has filed a
> lawsuit against the town of Laramie,
> Wyoming. The Church claims that the
> body of Jo Bailey belongs to the Church.
> The Church of Jo's building is located on
> Highland Boulevard only four blocks from
> the Church of Scientology. Coincidence?

This Article piqued my curiosity so I looked for other stories that might lend some light about what was talked about. I found the following story in the Laramie Boomerang Newspaper:

> At 3:30 yesterday afternoon, Mrs. Trundle
> of 8 Elm Avenue, in Centennial noticed a
> strange smell that came from the house
> next door. She knocked, but no one
> answered. "I know a man lives there," she
> told the sheriff. The door was forced open
> and a man found dead inside. Mr. Trundle
> identified the man as her neighbor Larry.

Because the death was suspicious, the
body was moved to the coroner's office in
Laramie. An autopsy found that the man
had died suddenly because of an embolism
in his brain. His finger prints were sent to
the FBI for identification. The FBI
announced that the dead man was Jo
Bailey, the author and religious figure.

No next of kin is known. He will be buried
in a public plot at the Laramie Cemetery.

About the same time that pro-bono lawyer I knew
asked me to join the lawsuit against the Chicago Hospital of Psychiatric Care on behalf of Joy Hope Luxlishski, the claimed daughter of Jo Bailey. Among
others named as plaintiffs in that suit included the
publisher of Jo Bailey's second book.

A hearing held and the Superior Court in the
county of Cook, Illinois, ruled that the hospital failed to
prove that Ms. Luxlishski was incompetent. She was
ordered immediately freed from her involuntary con-
finement.

I received email from her a few days later. In part
that email said, "I will take a bus to Laramie tomorrow
to try to get that DNA test done. I wanted to thank you
for taking my side."

The suit against Laramie, Wyoming to take custody of Jo Bailey's body was unopposed. The Church Of
Jo presented to the judge a letter written by Jo Bailey
himself and mailed to them before his death. The letter
read:

My ghost visited again, so close I could
touch her. And at long last I could hear her
clearly. She simply said, 'I forgive you.'

Then she vanished, I suspect for good, and in that moment I foresaw my own death. I will drop to the floor while I prepare fish. Then I will be among men in yellow robes who surround a brain in a jar. They will insert a needle into the brain and withdrew some brain matter. I will stand over a woman who kneels at a grave. The grave stone will be etched with my name. The woman will weep. Next my books will dumped in a huge pile and burned. I believe the Church of Jo must have my body. I don't know why.

Much evidence was presented to show that Jo Bailey could actually foresee events following death. The representatives of the church showed that their color was yellow.

In part, the judge ruled, "I have never seen such a flimsy display of evidence. But because no one opposes the suit, and because no rights or funds are claimed, only the body, I hereby rule that the body of the man known as Jo Bailey belongs to the Church of Jo."

The judge also ruled that all costs of de-internment and restoration of the burial plot, transportation and storage must be borne by the Church. The City of Laramie had no objection once they understood the ruling wouldn't cost them one dime.

Events Of 1982
Dahlia Phillips

Her journal written prior to her suicide

<u>Saturday</u>

I was surprised Jo remembered me. After that party in '68 it was like he had vanished from the surface of the Earth. We'd had a fling on a mattress on the top floor of that big house in Berkeley that smelled like burned popcorn. He was gone when I woke up with a terrible hangover. A month later I found out I was pregnant. His kid, I'm sure.

I couldn't keep the baby. My folks wouldn't let me. My dad was okay but my mom was furious. So I gave birth in a hospital in Berkeley, kept my daughter for a month then finally had to give her up for adoption. A girl, my daughter. I named her Joy because that name started with J O for Jo.

Last night I met Jo at an art opening in Pasadena. I took over an hour to get there by city bus. The second bus didn't think I had a good transfer but I begged and he let me on anyway. The art place was on a corner across from a park. I must have gotten there early because the big room wasn't crowded. I felt under-dressed in a clean blouse and my twice taken in and once mended gray dress slacks, still too big, held up with a belt, but I figured, what the heck, I'd been invited.

I knew Jo at once because of all the times he's shown up in the news. His hair was longer, of course, but still brown. And he wore a suit. I didn't expect that.

Hi, he said to me. You look too thin.

Hi, I said to him and say no I'm still too chubby.

I know you, he said. He looked me up and down. Then he said, You're from Berkeley. You're Dahlia. Not that exactly, of course. But something like that.

Yeah, I said to him. Then I asked him if he was there to look at the art? Course I wasn't there for the art myself, I told him, I was there for the free cheese and fruit plates.

Jo said, he was there because the artist made art from his books. I wish I could talk like Jo. He actually said words prettier than that. But I don't remember exactly how.

All these years I wanted to tell Jo about the baby, but when the time came I wasn't so sure at all. I wondered if I should tell him proud or blame him or maybe say it matter of fact. I must have thought about my words too long because he got a look on his face like he expected me to say something.

So I blurted everything out. I told Jo he had a daughter and that seemed to surprise him. Maybe shocked is closer. His eyes went wide and he stared at me. Then he calmed down and patted my arm. A warm pat, sure, but still just a pat.

Let's meet for lunch tomorrow, he said. He suggested that new Mexican place on Hollywood Boulevard. That was okay with me, so we made, well, a date.

Jo said something to the lady in charge of the art show. She wore a black dress that looked like it cost more money than I got in welfare in a year. She filled a bag, an actual cloth bag, with the most yummy stuff you ever ate and let me take everything home. The bag was empty and my stomach full by the time I got home on the bus. Made me sick though, I threw up all the good food. The bag was a nice cloth though, maybe for me to store old clothes.

<u>My Sunday Lunch with Jo, June 6 maybe?</u>

I think he chose that place on Hollywood Boulevard because of that big fountain in the back with all the tables. You can talk there and nobody can hear you because of the water noise from the fountain, real private. Lot's of stars are supposed to eat there, or that's what they tell you. I believe because of all the famous photos on the walls.

Jo paid for lunch. He had a big wad of twenties in his pocket. Weird, you know, because he dressed so poor all the time in his pictures. He wore blue jeans and a sweat shirt for lunch, not the suit he wore at the art show. I don't think the place wanted to let him in, but they believed he was famous so they did.

A heavy set man sat at the table next to us. I figured he was there to protect Jo. The man would watch everyone that came by. Even the waiters. I think he had a gun bulge under his sport coat. He dressed better than Jo too.

Jo asked about his daughter. Our daughter, I guess, but I was the one who gave her up.

He wanted to know how to find her. I told him that he couldn't because those records were sealed.

I'll find her he told me. He seemed really certain. But I didn't think he could.

I asked him if he could really listen to the dead?

No, he told me. I visit the memories of the dead, in the next life after you die and are reborn.

I asked him how that was different.

When you die, he said. You come back again but you're different. Maybe you're born from somebody else or you're a boy and not a girl. You live the beginning over again, but a little different. And those memories are not really memories, you know. More like you're reborn into another someplace else, I think he used the word dimension.

His talk made my head spin so I fingered the edge of the table cloth for something to hang onto. A simple stitch made by a machine, straight and even; made me feel calm, that stitch under my fingers.

The waiter came by then and asked if we wanted drinks. I ordered a strawberry daiquiri. Jo didn't order a drink.

I looked up and smiled. He waited for me. I can't kiss you if you drink that, he said.

I asked him why, don't you like drunks?

He smiled. You know, he said. I'm allergic to strawberries.

I'd forgotten. Or maybe I never knew. I mean we'd only been together one night. I couldn't think of anything to say to that.

So he told me about his mom. She was killed when he was a little boy. She was shot when she came home and found someone robbing the place. I couldn't save her, he says. Naturally I think of the crazy guy with a blanket for a cape. How he said he could save me.

But then Jo said, in her next life, the one that she lived again after she died, his mom never got married.

I asked him how he could tell if he visited someone reborn.

You can't, he told me. You and me might be reborn. And not only that, you can be reborn over and over again. And each time you change a little or a lot.

I was confused, of course, but I wanted to look like I understood. I struggled. I held onto the table cloth with my right hand, held and twisted. I asked him how he knew his mother didn't get shot in her next life?

I visit her, he said. Then he surprised me. He asked, You want me to show you?

I said sure but I wasn't sure.

Jo leaned back and closed his eyes. The bodyguard shook his head, like he'd seen Jo do this before.

I expected maybe a seance. You know, he would speak in a spooky voice like some dead guy. But no. He talked in his own voice. Calm like. Like he was really there.

I'll try to write down all his words, but I'm sure I'll miss some.

He said, My mom's in a grocery store. She's picks up oranges and hefts each in her hand. She puts some back. She puts some in a bag.

Man I wish I could talk like Jo. Sure I try to write down what I hear him say but everything comes out like my words. I don't have his words. But I gotta write something because I think what he told me is important.

Then he says, his mom doesn't recognize him of course, because in the next life she only had a daughter. She has no wedding ring on her finger. Jo says, She is younger than me, of course, because she died when I was in grammar school. So her memory, her new birth, started when I was already eight years old.

Hi ma'am, Jo says to her. Hi, she says to him. Jo asks, can I ask why you weigh each oranges?

Sure, the woman, his mother says.

Jo says, I like her smile. My mom was really pretty when she was younger.

His mother says, I weigh each one in my hand. The heavy ones have more juice. Usually the ones with the smooth skin have the most juice, but not all the time.

Even though his voice is there the whole time, I can tell when he talks and when his mom is talks.

You would think, he tells me. He talked to me as himself again and that surprised me. He said, That if your whole life memory is there when you die, your whole life memory would exist in your next life. I can visit the past memories of my dead mom, but not the future ones. Because she hasn't lived them yet.

The waiter came then and set down my drink. I thought I shouldn't drink, but I did anyway. Jo let me order anything I wanted. I ordered the salad because of the walnuts. I wanted a tamale but I was watching my weight. Jo didn't order because he said he had a meeting. He waited until I got my food then paid and left.

God, I've been writing for hours. Amazing. I guess, easier to write when I actually did something. Go figure.

Events Of 1994
Ace Hoklins

Father Bob Hoklins, The Church of Jo, Los Angeles, California

That following weekend Mr. Scallody sent three of the guys out to the Mojave to take care of Jo Bailey. Larry drove and Frank King took the rifle. Sam Datworthy went along to do anything that required strength. I stayed behind with Mr. Scallody and the other two.

The next day Mr. Scallody called us three together to tell us he had to run into L.A for the day. "If anyone comes around asking," he said. "Tell them I'll be back tonight."

But he never came back. The three guys from the Desert came back two days later, Larry driving of course. But Mr. Scallody never came back. We talked Larry into a drive down to L.A. to find out what happened. He came back that night and told us Mr. Scallody got himself shot and killed in a bar.

Seven guys with no boss shared cots in a warehouse by the train tracks in nowheresville. Naturally tempers flared. I personally broke up three fist fights. And the place started to stink. At the insistence of Evan Datworthy, we broke into Mr. Scallody's office and divided up the money we found there. Enough for all of us to get a fresh start. George Wriggles objected to an even split because he thought the Datworthy brothers should share a split. I pointed out that the brothers were totally different and did everything separately, so they should get one split each. That seemed to settle the matter.

I telephoned Father Desmond who acted pleased to hear from me. He reminded me he had only dropped me off four months earlier. I told him that Defoe Scallody had been killed and ask if he could pick me up and give me my job back. "I don't like that Defoe bunch," I told him. "They're all killers at heart."

"I'm sorry to hear that," he told me. "Of course. I would be delighted to have you back. I will pick you up tomorrow if that is okay?"

I told him, "Yes please," hung up, then went to find the other guys to find out what their plans were. I could only find George and Larry. Frank and the Datworthy brothers had already left.

"Where did they go?" I asked Larry the driver.

"The brothers got greedy," he said, and spit at the ground. "They said they planned to kidnap Jo Bailey for money. Them and that fool Frank after his fuckup in the Mojave."

"Did they tell you what they planned?"

George had stuffed his large duffle bag into the trunk of Larry's car. He wiped his hands on his pants and said, "If you can believe the brothers. Bigger liars than I've ever seen in my life."

Larry added, "They intended to hold him in an abandoned silver mine. Don't know where, but Evan said their dad left them ownership of one. I can't rightly say that's true or not." He shrugged.

Larry and George packed the car and drove off. Larry's parting words were, "Don't take any wooden nickels."

I waved and called, "I wooden think of it." Larry and George laughed. I watched their car pull to the road and turn right, and then it was gone.

That left me the afternoon to kill. I cleaned up the warehouse the best I could. I couldn't find a broom so I didn't sweep. But I did haul out all the trash and broke down and stacked all but one cot. I found a crowbar in a corner by the small bathroom. I broke into the office with all the news clips on the walls.

That office was the one with a broom. That figures. As long as I was in there I decided to pull down and throw away all the documentation. As I pulled each down I read as much as I could. Mr. Scallody had been sloppy. I found dozens upon dozens of documents that were about other people but that had been folded or cut to mask that fact. I quickly found a pattern to his lies and deception. The papers covering the walls fell like a house of cards. Marked cards I felt, used to cheat me. I packed the trash in bags. I managed to dodged a bullet. If Mr. Scallody had not died I might have been convinced to do something terrible.

After the walls were clean I rifled the drawers and found more money. A quarter of a million all total, in envelopes and paper bags. I said to the room, "You were well financed, weren't you?"

Too late I realized I should have left the papers on the wall to show Father Desmond. "Oh well," I said. "He'll have to be happy with a big donation to the church." And that made me smile.

I worked again as a gardener for a whole year. During that time I bought and read both of Jo Bailey's books. I was impressed by his willingness to test his theories. His books had a scientific slant to religion I hadn't seen before. I tried to talk to Father Desmond about the books but he became furious and lumped Jo Bailey with Scientology and Satanism as fringe religions intended to steer the gullible away from belief in the true God.

I kept my thoughts about religion to myself after that and only talked with Father Desmond about his religion and my love of puzzles. That was a combination Father Desmond enjoyed. One day Father Desmond revealed to me he had enjoyed chess as a boy. We began to play chess on Saturdays. Over these leisurely games he would posit his thoughts to me in the form of questions like, "If there was no Hell and only a Heaven, what would prevent the spread of evil in the world?"

Father Desmond had a sneaky streak too. As a gift he got me a book of Bible crossword puzzles. That way I was forced to study the Bible in order to solve the puzzles.

After a year I began to feel like a permanent employee of the church. Unfortunately that was when news finally broke that Jo Bailey had been kidnapped. Father Desmond knew everything about what he called the "Scallody embarrassment." He found me in the garden. He carried a newspaper in his hand and a stern look on his face. "Ace," he said. "You have to contact the FBI with what you know. I know all that happened over a year ago, but your information may still be important."

I did and the FBI arrested me as a material witness. Father Desmond tried to prevent them from handcuffing me but failed. He asked them to wait as they loaded me into the back of a car. Father Desmond ran back into the church and emerged seconds later. "I had hoped to give you these for your birthday, but I suppose ahead of time will have to do." He handed me four books through the car window. The books were bound with a simple purple ribbon.

"What are they?" I asked. I held them on top of my lap with my handcuffed hands.

"The holy Bible, of course. A brand new book of crosswords for your birthday and the two Jo Bailey books I found hidden in your room." He said, with a wink. "I figure can't hurt you to hear the horse's mouth."

"Thank you for everything," I told him. "You've been like the Dad I never had."

Father Desmond smiled, but like he was embarrassed.

I told him, "Don't take and wooden nickels."
He laughed and said, "I won't."

Events of 1987-1998
Dustin Willowsmith

Reporter for the San Francisco Examiner, Reconstructed notes of several stories about Jo Bailey

A scant two weeks later, the radio said that Highland Boulevard was closed because crowds surrounded
the Church of Jo. Estimates put the number of mourners at over fifty thousand. By 10:00 a.m. they had
spilled from the sidewalks and began to fill the street.
By noon they had filled the street from side to side. I
headed out there to see for myself and used my press
credentials to park close.

A typical too-warm southern California day, the
crowd was loose and relaxed and well spaced so I could
move around. The Church grounds were surrounded
by high fences draped with flowing yellow cloth. Men in
yellow robes passed among the mourners handing out
bottled water and paper hats.

At two in the afternoon an unmarked white truck
pulled up to the edge of the crowd and thousands of
books were dumped from the back into a tall pile. Two
men visible in the back of the truck threw several lit
highway flares at the pile of books. But for some reason
the pile didn't catch on fire. The books were all copies
of Jo Bailey's books.

Many in the crowd became furious and chased
after the truck as, with a roar, the truck sped away. So
many people clogged the street and chased the truck
that the police could not follow in their cars.

I made my way over to the pile of books and
picked up one. That book smelled vaguely of gasoline.
Certainly not a strong enough smell to burn. I thumbed
through the book and found that each and every page

had a big X drawn through made with a wide black permanent marker. Soon, many people began to pluck books from the pile. They seemed to want them for souvenirs despite the way each was defaced.

I noticed one man smell a book like I had. He frowned then tried to light that book with a cigarette lighter. To his surprise the book caught. The man dropped the flaming book and jumped back. The book dropped to the pile and its flames caused the entire pile to begin to burn. I could feel the heat on my face.

A fire truck pulled up immediately and sounded its horn to make people back away from the fire. Within mere moment, the firemen put the fire out. Water pushed soggy books all over the street and created a significant mess.

At 3:00 p.m. the crowd grew quiet. In the distance a helicopter approach. An industrial helicopter appeared and hovered over the church. The crowd began to cheer and applaud. The helicopter settled behind wildly flapping yellow curtains and the crowd grew quiet again. A man from the Church emerged and stood high on the front steps of the church. He spoke on a megaphone.

"Please come back tomorrow. Tomorrow at 8:00 a.m. We will have an open coffin to view then. Please come back at eight."

Then the other men in yellow robes wove through the crowds and spoke the same message. The crowd slowly dispersed. Before I left I looked around and discovered that all the soggy burned books were gone. I noticed one woman walk away with a pile in her arms. Then I noticed another man toss a couple copies into the back seat of his car. I was glad I kept my copy. I began to think that book might be worth something some day after all.

On my drive home the news told me the evening commute on Highland Boulevard was opened again.

The next morning I arrived early expecting to beat the crowds. But at 7:00 a.m. I already found a long line of people leading into the church. Behind them, the line extended both ways up and down the sidewalk for many blocks. A local police officer told me, "Runs up to Hollywood Boulevard, then west for five blocks. The other way the crowd runs half mile in the direction of downtown. "We can't complain, though, the people are calm and well behaved," the policeman said.

I noticed men in yellow robes move along the lines pushing small carts. They handed out coffee and tea, sun screen, paper hats and doughnuts. I approached one as he came near.

"What's going on?"

"Don't you know. These people here wait to view the open casket of Jo Bailey. And they are all lay people, they don't even belong to the church."

"How did the church get founded? The first I knew of the church was in the news about the suit against Laramie."

He peered at my press credentials. "You're Dustin Willowsmith? I think I know that name. Please, please, come inside. There's someone you must meet."

I followed him past the line and through the front door of the church. Inside looked more like a hotel lobby than the entry to a church. I followed him down a well lit side corridor to an office. "Please," he told me. "Have a seat. He'll be with you soon."

I had to only wait for a few minutes. Another man in yellow robes entered. His robes looked tailored and much more expensive. He introduced himself as, "First Member Bob Hoklins." he was clean cut with short hair and wore horned rimmed glasses.

I explained why I was there and that news tickled his funny bone.

He laughed, then began. "I and four others formed the Church of Jo in 1998. Jo Bailey gave us ten million dollars to begin. I met him once, but the others never did. The money came from a bank in the Philippines. We, like everyone, thought he had hidden there. We were as surprised as anyone when he was found dead in Centennial, Wyoming."

"Why did you sue the City of Laramie?"

"I don't know how much you know about our religion." He paused.

"Not much."

"Our main belief is that life exists after death in the form of rebirth into other dimensions. You can think of reincarnation with a twist. Instead of a rebirth as usual, you are reborn elsewhere."

I nodded.

"But one strange property of memories is that they take a finite amount of time to exit the brain. So if the brain is destroyed too fast, like in an explosion, the memories are lost. The person vanishes as if he or she never existed. So you see the importance for us to possess the body. We had to show the world that Jo Bailey's brain was intact. We had to demonstrate, with the physical, the continuance of the metaphysical."

"So his head is open in the coffin so folks can see his brain?"

"Not exactly. The body is intact. The brain has been removed and placed in a jar. That jar occupies the central and most precious place in the core of our Church."

"How gruesome."

"I can see how you might think so." He laughed again. "But come." He rose. "There's someone you must meet."

He led me down another hallway to another door. The door was closed so he knocked. An unexpectedly large door opened and a woman peered out.

"I present Joy Hope Luxlishski."

She was smaller and older than I expected. Her long blonde hair framed a squarish face. She smiled and extended her hand and we shook. She said,

191

"Thank you for your help. I couldn't sue the hospital without your help. I would still be locked up there."

The First Member then said, "Joy, or so we believe, might be the actual daughter of Jo Bailey. That's a fact we test the after tomorrow. Think you can stay around for that?"

I apologized and explained I must travel north for a food story on the restaurants of Napa. My own excuse struck me as lame, but that was the truth.

Joy thanked me again and hugged me. "Be sure to leave me your number in case I need to get in touch with you."

I gave her my card, then the First Member led me out and past the open coffin. I stood for moment and watched. Every person that viewed his body wept. Without exception. None acted like gawkers. All of them seemed unusually sincere.

Events Of 1982
Dahlia Phillips

Her journal written prior to her suicide

Two days later. Monday.

I got scared and had to stop writing. Outside feels extra dark tonight. Maybe I am a chicken, but Jo really scared me that day. No nightmares though. I keep my fingers crossed. But I'm okay for a while. The sun is out. We're supposed to meet again next Saturday at the same restaurant. I got some fabric in the closet, I think I'll make new dress for next time. I hope I have a pattern because I don't have enough money to buy one.

Yippe! Tuesday!

Tuesday is Red's Tamale Day! I had Jo's leftover salad for dinner and then again for breakfast. Maybe I was sick because of all the walnuts or maybe the cheese bits, I don't know, but I had a scary dream last night. Not a nightmare, spooky. I was at the art show and every time the person with the food walked by a painting, the person in the painting reached out and took the food. They took huge helpings but couldn't eat any food because their mouths were sewn shut. I really saw everything happen but nobody else did. Weird.

Saturday Lunch With Jo

Jo says he can take me with him to visit reborn people if I want.
I ask him how.

He tells me to hold his hand.

Like a Vulcan mind meld, I ask.

He says no. He tells me to hold his hand again. So I do.

Strange so I will try to say exactly what he said, even though I don't understand a word all.

I don't visit next lives as me, he says. I inhabit other people. That's the word he used. Inhabit. I won't forget that word, inhabit. It really bothered me.

You'll see, he says. Just close your eyes. So I do.

I was a nurse. I looked at myself and I was dressed like a nurse. A real sensation, I tell you, like I really was a nurse.

I looked around and we're in a pale-green hospital room, and a doctor holds a newborn baby in a blue and white striped blanket, and a woman lays on the delivery table covered in a sheet. I didn't recognize the woman.

Jo spoke to me in his Jo voice. But the doctor speaks instead.

A fine baby girl, says Jo the doctor. What do you want to name her? He asked the girl in the bed.

Samantha, the mother says. Because my husband's father was named Sam.

I think I got all that right. Yeah. That's what Jo said.

I let go of Jo's hand and I still sat at the table. I'm sure I looked a fright. I adjusted my skirt. I made a mistake when I adjusted the waist and the front rides up when I sit. I asked him how he did that.

I can inhabit people in the next life, he says. That word again. Inhabit.

I can inhabit non-human memories too, he says. You want to see? He smiled a big smile like he was about to do something really special.

I ask him what he means, like animals or plants?

Aliens, he says.

Like Star Trek? I ask. Or like when we got stoned back then? You remember, like our first LSD trip. When I lived inside insect people.

Yes, he says. Just like that only different, hold my hand.

I do and, one minute I sat at the table with Jo, the next moment I'm huge and transparent and I float. I try to look around but can't, not like I'm blind, instead I can "feel light" instead of see. And I feel Jo a long ways off.

Can you hear me? He asks, but not in words, in colors. I find this hard to explain.

I'm not sure how, but I feel warmth from him, but the warmth has shapes. The shapes have meaning. They mean, can you feel my words?

I try to say words back but don't have a mouth. Instead bubbles inside me move and warm up my huge skin. I feel like a gigantic billboard. I try to say, yes.

Then I feel heat from below. At first the heat is so far away I can ignore the threat. But the heat starts to rise. The heat searched for me from way down there and noticed me way above. Like a shark circles below and looks up for a fish. A big heat, and it continued to rise toward me. I mean a heat lots bigger than I am and I'm huge. But the thing, the heat, was still a long ways off but still rose towards me. I felt danger. I got really scared and try to let go of Jo's hand, but I don't have any hands so I can't.

I feel comforting colors from Jo and I start to calm down. He sends warm signals to me that say, look inside at the life in you.

I look, but not with eyes of course. My body is huge. Huge like the Goodyear blimp. But I somehow see things that live inside me. Flying things, like I have a whole city inside me.

I try to send warm words to the things inside but they ignore me.

I floated there for a long time and watched the huge heat rise underneath me. The heat continued to rise for a long time but must have been really far away because the threat still seemed a long ways below.

After a while I grew aware of other things like me and Jo. Hundreds or maybe even thousands of them. Some so far away I could barely feel their warmth at all.

Then, like that, I was back at the table. I could see and speak again. I must have been shaking because Jo asked me if I was okay.

I tell him no. I ask him not to do that anymore.

Events Of 1994
Ace Hoklins

Father Bob Hoklins, The Church of Jo, Los Angeles,
California

The FBI sped me off then, to the airport. From
there I was flown to Sacramento and there I was put
into a car again. On the airplane they uncuffed me so I
could read. I also read in the car, a ride that wound
from Sacramento all the way up past Nevada City then
up a long series of switchbacks into dense trees and
eventually down a gravel road. At the end, around an
old mine entrance, we pulled in and parked, where a
dozen police and an ambulance were loosely laid out.
By then I had compared first two of Jo Bailey's books to
the Bible and found Jo Bailey the more convincing.

A uniformed policeman with a narrow face
walked up and opened the car door. A cold breeze and
pine. I realized I was high in the mountains. The policeman bent and looked at me. "You Hoklins?" he asked.

I nodded and set my book down.

"We need you to identify some bodies."

"Some?" I asked.

"Two," he said.

I followed him around to a low, black morgue van
I handn't noticed parked beside the ambulance. The
back door of the van was open and two bodies in black
plastic bags lay side by side like two fallen pawns. The
policeman zipped open the first, the one with a smaller
body.

"Frank Kings," I said. Frank had a bullet hole in
his forehead.

The policeman nodded like he already knew the name. He zipped the first bag closed and unzipped the second one with the larger body.

"Sam Datworthy," I said. "Where's his brother Evan?"

The policeman nodded again. He zipped the second bag closed and said, "Follow me."

Sam looked so innocent as he laid there with his eyes closed. That poor big dumb muscle man. I thought of him back there in the morgue van and felt angry. I blamed his brother.

We entered the mine. The opening was taller and wider than I expected, not at all claustrophobic. If felt like I was walking into one of the black squares in a crossword puzzle. The squares between all words, the square without meaning. I asked as we walked, "What happened."

"Those two guys," the policeman indicated behind us with his thumb. "They were outside guarding when we arrived. They fired at us, so we fired back. Killed them both."

The policeman rounded a turn and stopped.

I stopped too. A man lay on the ground, pinned there by a massive fallen wooden beam. A small tire jack lay abandoned next to the beam. "Hi Ace," the man said to me and chuckled.

"Hi Evan," I said. Although I wanted to be angry with him because of his brother, I couldn't. He looked too pathetic lying there pinned by a huge log, his face ashen. The best I could muster was, "Checkmated huh? Too bad about what you did to your brother."

"I figure you were the one who ratted on us."

I looked at him and realized he wanted me to feel guilt. But I wasn't about to accept guilt for what he did. I studied him. He appeared to be in pain but was resisting showing pain to the policeman. The beam on his leg looked really heavy. "I had to do the right thing,"

I told him. "If you had read Jo Bailey's books you'd know I was right."

"Yeah maybe," he said.

The policeman asked me, "You identify him as Evan Datworthy?"

"Yeah," I said. "That's him."

Evan watched me for a moment then said, "Your Jo Bailey was wrong you know."

"How's that?"

"He told me I would be buried alive. But all that happened was a wooden beam fell on my leg."

A man in a suit walked up and spoke to the policeman. "The engineer has arrived," he said. "He wants everyone out. He told us that in old mines even a single fallen beam can weaken the whole structure."

The policeman next to me said, "We gotta go."

I turned to follow the other two out. Behind me Evan yelled, "Hey! What about me? What about me?"

The policeman called over his shoulder, "We'll be back for you when that hydraulic jack arrives."

Outside in the sunshine and fresh air the FBI man that flew with me walked over. "Jo Bailey wants to see you," he said.

"Jo Bailey?"

"Yeah. He was the one who was kidnapped. They held him in a cage at the back."

"Sure," I said. "I'll meet the man."

We walked up hill toward the back of all the parked cars. They were all black I realized, scattered like checkers or dominos. We arrived at a large sedan with tinted windows. Just as we got there the ground began to shake.

"What's that?" I asked.

The FBI man turned and looked at the mine. "A cave-in," he said.

I looked too and watched a huge plume of rock grey smoke billow out of the mine. The large black square smudged out by a dense fog and vanished. The rumble faded. As the dust settled and the vibration stopped, I could see that the opening had collapsed shut. "Checkmate," I said again.

"Damn," said the FBI man. "That guy was still pinned in there."

Behind me a car door opened. I turned. A brown haired, older man grey at the temples leaned out. His face was dirty, he appeared a tad thin, and he needed a shave. "Hi," he said to me. "I'm Jo Bailey. I'd like to talk with you if I may."

I was glad to get into the car with him. The air around the mine started to take on a bitter flavor with a gritty aftertaste from the death of Evan. I sat and closed the door and marveled at the quiet. As if buried into a tomb, that sudden and that still.

"I'm Ace Hoklins," I said. And as I said that, I realized the name Ace had taken on a foreign sound to me. Ace was the name I had taken in my twenties to prove I was tough. Like a card discovered up my sleeve, phoney and wrong. "I was originally Bob, but I changed my name into Ace. I think I'll change back again."

"While you stood outside the door I sensed something in you."

I was immediately on guard. "You mean like I'll die?"

Jo Bailey laughed. "No, not death. Something else." He closed his eyes. "I see yellow cloth billow in a light breeze. The yellow is soft like a summer's sunlight. I see you walk out of a church door with blood on your face. I hear alarm bells. You won't be blown up." He opened his eyes. "Mean anything to you?"

I remembered Father Desmond, but his robe was black. "No," I said. "Nothing at all."

"Have you read my books?"

I smiled at that. "Yes."

"And what do you think?"

"You're not a killer."

He laughed again. "That's a common misconception. I even fooled myself for a while. I've often wondered why I can foresee death but can never prevent it? Like I'm wired into a time that must be. Yet in all other actions I feel totally free and effectual."

I laughed. "You should have seen Scallody's office. As if a tornado had plastered the wall with lies."

Jo smiled. "I like your sense of imagery. Would you considered joining the Church of Jo?"

"I didn't know such a church existed yet."

Jo chuckled. "Not yet." He looked at me seriously for a moment as if he had pre-gauged my reaction ahead of time. Then he added, "I thought maybe the Church should exist and I thought that you might be a good person to help found a new church."

I opened my mouth to say something but didn't. I wanted to tell him he was crazy or a lunatic, but I hesitated. I think I might actually have wanted to hear him out. I finally managed to ask "What?"

"I'm sorry. I didn't mean to spring that on you out of the blue like that. I have considered setting up a church for a while. That and whether or not to write a third book." He held both hands palms up. "A tossup in a way. In truth I don't think enough people have read my books for the books alone to do the job. To spread my ideas, that is, to change the way people think about death."

"What makes you think a church will do a better job?"

Jo smiled. "Personnel," he said. "A church would have the personnel to spread my observations more widely. A book cannot carry itself to another country to convince. A book is words on a page. A book is inanimate, a thing, not a person. People motivate people. A book is a tool. Think of the bible. It would have just been a book, without Christian churches to promote it."

I leaned back and looked at him. He appeared sincere, and he didn't seem at all preachy. He was a man. A man with a strange story to tell. "Let me tell you a story," I said. "About another man that tried to motivate people." I told him about DeFoe Scallody and his mission to kill Jo. He interrupted me only once to question a date, but otherwise listened politely.

"Like I said," he told me when I finished. "People are best to convince people."

"True," I said. I pictured the Presbyterian Church in Gilroy and its huge buildings, its exquisite woodwork, and vast parking lot and grounds. "But wouldn't building a church cost an awful lot?"

That one remark caused Jo to smile the most broadly of all. "Money," he said, and shook his head at me. "Is no problem."

"I'd have to change my name back to Bob."

He half reached to take my hand. "Do we have a deal?"

I hesitated. I don't know why. Perhaps because of all my Christian talks with Father Desmond. Perhaps I feared being responsible for something new. I didn't know. I didn't have anyone to ask. "Would you mind if I talk your proposal over with Father Desmond?"

He extended his hand further and smiled again. "Sure," he said. "I wouldn't want you to proceed in any other way. Let's shake to seal the deal."

We shook hands, then he added, "These glimpses of a future that I see. . . ."

I let his hand go and waited.

"I see you in them as part of the church. That's why I don't feel like I have to do a lot of convincing. There will be a church and you'll be part of that church and nothing I do can prevent that."

His statement felt odd to me. Like a paradox. "What if I turn you down?"

He smiled, genuinely happy. "You won't. But don't decide right away. Take your time. Consider carefully. Talk with your Father Desmond."

I thanked him again but didn't turn him down. He offered to drive me down the mountain. But the FBI man opened my door then and said, "Ace Hoklins, I need to take your statement. For the record."

Jo's car drove off while I dictated my statement. I surprised myself by not feeling bad about Frank or the Datworthy brothers. They killed themselves. All I did was keep them from harming a good man.

Events of 1987-1998
Dustin Willowsmith

Reporter for the San Francisco Examiner, Reconstructed notes of several stories about Jo Bailey

I was in Napa when Joy telephoned to tell me about the explosion. I couldn't think of anything to say so I told her how sorry I was. I was still in Napa because the story I was writing had expanded to include all the small towns from Napa north to Santa Rosa. Who could have imagined so many good restaurants existed up there? I was still stuck there when the funeral was held for the dead priests.

My only regret was that I couldn't report on the explosion myself. The slow but inevitable decline of newspapers had lead to a shedding of reporters into trades they wouldn't have considered before. I wanted to leave my food beat and report on the hard news of the Church of Jo, but I couldn't.

When I got back to my desk at the LA Times I found a postcard propped up on my keyboard. Greg, my former editor at the San Francisco Examiner, had sent the card. Only one sentence had been written like a horizontal line, "I see you finally found Jo Bailey." I laughed and turned the card over to look at the photo on the front. A photograph a metal bridge over railroad tracks, where the label read, "Laramie, Wyoming."

I taped the postcard to the top of my computer monitor. A reminder of the days lost during which I could write hard news. I glanced at the postcard then began my story about the restaurants of the town of Sonoma.

The LA Times to downsize me out of a job again quicker than I expected. I decided to move back to San Francisco and start that cookbook I had always planned to. But before I left I stopped by the Church of Jo one last time. Joy was up north with a benefactor so I visited with Bob Hoklins. I noticed right away his robes no longer looked tailored. In fact they looked rather shabby and stained. He noticed my stare and explained, "After the explosion I did not want to dishonor the dead by renewing my clothing and going on. I decided to wear the same robes I wore during the explosion until they become threadbare and fall off of me. Only then will I consider anything new."

"I've been let go from the Times and will move back to San Francisco."

"We plan to open a church there next."

"Really?"

"Would you find it okay if we looked you up when we do?"

"I'd be grateful." I thought a moment then added, "I'll be writing a cookbook, so maybe I'll be able to test some recipes on you."

"Say," he said. "You want to see Jo's brain?"

"I thought that was all destroyed in the explosion."

He laughed and said, "Follow me." He led me down a short corridor and down a few steps into a circular room. "The explosion toppled and cracked the jar but the brain survived mostly intact."

In the center of the circular room was a pedestal and atop the pedestal a cylindrical clear jar and inside the jar a brain.

I stepped forward and peered at the brain. "Looks like a regular brain."

"That it does." He waved his arm to indicate the wall.

Three horizontal rows of letters covered the walls. Each row of letters was separated from the next by a thin gray horizontal line.

Hoklins indicated the top row, "That is a normal person's DNA. Below that is Jo's DNA and below that is Joy's DNA."

I studied the three rows. The bottom two rows had a sequence of letters highlighted in red. I compared the red areas to the corresponding area in the top row. They were different. I asked, "What's all that mean?"

"The sequence in red appears the same in Jo and Joy, but doesn't correspond to normal DNA. We think that is the source of their powers."

I tried to recall what I knew about DNA. "You mean that some day you might be able to make another Jo?"

"Maybe," he said, with a wry smile. "Maybe we will."

Back in San Francisco and months later I watched an afternoon TV show about Chef Gibions desire to bring quality foods to retirement homes. The announcer mentions a new movement called, "Slow Foods." The story mentioned that Chef Gibions would be at the Cabbage Valley Retirement Center in Walnut Creek that coming Friday afternoon. I had begun my cookbook and realized quotations from real chefs might help sell the book.

Jo grew up in Concord east of Walnut Creek. So I thought I might kill two birds with one stone. Friday morning, I visited the Hall of Records in Concord's new City Hall. In a temporary trailer out back, I stood among faded documents in boxes, papers waited to be digitally scanned. One file mentioned Jo's parents. The file said, they had sued a Dr. Scallody. Evidently, the doctor had been a quack who drilled a hole in the back of Jo's skull.

In a water-stained file with a sticker that partly read, "Rescued from the flood of '75," I found a hand written account, signed by a Simon Bailey, who I assumed could be Jo's father.

Jerome Scallody pretended, with criminal intent, to be a doctor and set up a private office in the hills above Oakland. He offered to free the trapped souls of insane children by drilling a hole in the back of the head and shocking the soul free using electricity.

In 1953 without my permission or knowledge, my wife took our son, Jo Bailey, to Dr. Scallody for treatment. When I next saw my son, a spot on the top back of his head had been shaved. A bandage covered a hole about the diameter of a pencil. The hole had been filled with a silver substance that resembled tooth filling.

Jo was never the same after his treatment. Before the treatment he was an outgoing and friendly six year old. I believed his earlier vivid descriptions of other worlds had been due to his imagination. His mother believed he was troubled, or even possessed, and needed treatment.

Joe is quiet and withdrawn. He still has fun with his friends, but won't talk to his mother.

I sat there and held that stained sheet of paper. The trailer was cramped and smelled a bit moldy. At

207

the other end, by the open door, a young man in an orange team-shirt copied documents with a steady click, click using a large grey machine.

I recalled how Jo said in his first book he believed that the hole in his head gave him his powers. "Damn," I said.

The document was signed by Simon Bailey and had a faded notarized seal below that. I set that piece aside to copy and stretched to work our a few kinks. The windows behind me were open and when I didn't hear copier I heard birds through them. Chirpy birds, maybe blackbirds, but I couldn't see them because the windows were opaque.

I leaned over again, got busy and rummaged through more papers. I found a newspaper article. The article said, Jo Bailey's parents, Simon and Amanda Bailey had sued Dr. Scallody and tried to put him out of business. The settlement was in their favor and they netted two-hundred thousand dollars. I estimated in my head that would be nearly two million in current money. I whistled which caused the boy to look at me which interrupted his click-click rhythm. I nodded at him and listened to the birds again, then returned to my search duty.

Divorce papers surfaced which showed that Jo's dad, Simon, had divorced his wife soon after that law suit. Simon had moved to Charleston, South Carolina. Amanda continued to raise Jo in their same house, until her death. According to her death certificate, she had died of a gunshot wound to the head.

Events Of 1982
Dahlia Phillips

Her journal written prior to her suicide

Tuesday I think. Still June.

I forgot to keep up my diary. Sorry me.

Jo called me last night. On the phone he says he knows a guy who knows a guy who can find adopted-away kids.

I tell him that isn't possible. I tell him I'm still shaking from being a floating thing.

He tells me he has a ghost.

I ask him what that means.

He tells me about the girl who drowned. I think he said her name was Esther.

He tells me he sees her. Then he says, I can't find her next life anywhere. I can't inhabit her.

I ask him what he means. But I also notice he said he couldn't inhabit her.

Jo said, he didn't know. She visits him every once in a while. Always from far off. He said, yesterday he was sitting on the edge of the pool when she appeared.

That's right, he said pool. And he met me at a restaurant. Doesn't that burn you?

Anyway, she appeared far off by the trees that lined his back yard. She was in front of the trees. But he still couldn't see her face clearly.

I ask him why not.

Maybe, he tells me. Maybe he still carried too much guilt. I wondered guilt about what. But then he said, that maybe he couldn't see her, not when she was unwilling to show herself.

I think I got that right.

Next Jo says she stood there for about a minute or two and he smelled strawberries, then she faded away. Like she dissolved in a movie.

I ask him if that scared him.

He says no, not scared. More sad. And a little lonely. I miss her, he says to me. After all, she was my first love.

I'm sure that's what he said. His first love. After that remark I wished he'd hang up, but I didn't say that to him. Instead I asked if she was a ghost because she drowned.

He was silent then. I guess he though I asked something stupid and I probably did. But I couldn't think of anything smart to say, and I wondered about that. So I stayed quiet too.

After a while he said, he was sorry to have bothered me.

I told him that was okay.

He said, he'd let me know if he found Joy.

I think he means happiness, then I remember my lost daughter. I tell him not to let me know.

He says okay, then bye and hangs up. Rude like.

I wonder about Esther his ghost and that she drowned. I wonder if drowning means Jo can't inhabit her.

Friday, June 25 still 1982

Sorry diary, I forgot to write again. I have been thinking about Jo. Not good thoughts. Just worried about him. I don't know why.

I tried to visit the next lives of the dead, but can't do that without him. I tried to score some LSD from the guy on the corner. But he wanted to charge me too much. I thought that LSD might make it possible like before to visit the next life. Oh well, but that's okay. Or maybe its not okay, I don't know.

I still have nightmares. Mostly I'm one of those big things, with the huge heat below that rose up to get me. That scared the bejesus out of me every time. I woke up covered in sweat, and all my bed covers were on the floor.

I think that if I can visit those floating things again everything will be okay. But Jo's phone is disconnected and there's no numbers listed for him. I worry about him. I worry about me too. I worry I might drink again. Maybe.

Wednesday in November

Thanksgiving is next week so I try calling my cousin Bob using the pay phone at the gas station. His phone, you know the one that will always be good, answered with a message. The message said, his department was closed to save tax players money. I don't pay taxes so I thought that was a bad idea. I left a message for him and hope. Anyway I miss him and wonder where he's got to.

I'm afraid of everything these days. I don't want to die because Jo will be able to inhabit me. Get inside me and make me say things. And if he can get inside me, maybe he can read my mind. That would be sick. Really sick.

So I'm really careful. But I'm jumpy too. A car can honk its horn a block away and I'll jump out of my skin. I wish I could afford that LSD.

Friday, December 17, 1982

I got a letter saying I lost my welfare and I'm not sure what I'll do. My neighbor across the hall thinks I can get disability, but I don't think so. That would mean I am crazy, and I'm not. I'm afraid that I'll drink again.

It's all Jo Bailey's fault. He haunted my brain and all I can think about is that damn big heat below me. That and Jo reading my mind. I hate him. I hate him for what he did to me.

<u>Sunday I think. Yeah must be. December?</u>

Hi diary. I drank again last night. I woke up feeling sick and found I'd peed all over the bed. I dreamed I was drowning and somehow felt safe. Jo couldn't inhabit me if I drown, he couldn't get inside my head if I drown. I'd be a ghost like Esther. A ghost he couldn't inhabit.

<u>Hey, Tuesday. Red's Tamale Day.</u>

I need to wash the sheets. I wish my clothes weren't too big. I need another drink. But what's the point. What's the point of a diary? What I really need are rocks. Big rocks, like those in the garden and big pockets like in my raincoat, my too big raincoat made of cloth so I can sew it shut.

Goodbye diary. Goodbye cousin Bob. Goodbye Jo. Goodbye Joy wherever you are, I love you and wish I could have been with you always. I'm a terrible mother. I gave my daughter away. What monster mother does that? Oops, broke the pencil, have to keep writing in pen. Well I'm done writing anyway. I'm sick to my stomach, didn't sleep well. Damn nightmares. Damn Jo.

Hey, I counted my money and I have enough for a small bottle of cheap vodka and a bus ride to the beach. Tuesday again. It's Red's Tamale Day. I wish I had enough for a tamale too.

Newspaper Clipping
Los Angeles Times
Wednesday, December 22, 1982

The body of one Dahlia Phillips was found washed up on the beach north of Malibu in the early morning by two teenage boys. Police reported the victim's coat pockets were filled with stones and sewn shut. Her coat had to be cut open to try to revive her because it too was sewn shut. The police believed she committed suicide. A note wrapped in plastic, and safety pinned to her coat, read simply, "I am a ghost."

Events Of 1994
Ace Hoklins

Father Bob Hoklins, The Church of Jo, Los Angeles,
California

A week later, I found Father Desmond violently opposed to the church idea. "Are you sure you want to be involved with a crackpot cult?" he asked me.

The sunlight made him glow that afternoon. I stood there and talked to a real man of faith about my intent to found a new religion. That seemed, well plain wrong. No not wrong, perhaps silly. "I wouldn't be asking you," I said. "But you are the closest thing to a paternal father I ever had. You are the one man I can actually talk to. I need to make things that last, to create something. I've been too destructive for too long. Does that make sense?"

He stepped closer and put his hand on my shoulder. His touch felt oddly powerful, as if his hand channeled more than himself. He smiled a calming caring smile and said, "I bless you no matter what you do. You, Ace, are more important to me than anything you may do. Even anything as foolish as starting a fringe church, and I wish you wouldn't. But I know I cannot stop you if you chose to. But you. I bless you and will always bless you, Ace, my friend."

I wanted to fall to my knees and kiss that hand, but I stood there, somehow strengthened by his blessing. "Thanks," I said. Then I added with a smile, "Thank you a million times over, Father."

And the rest, as they say, was history. Jo phoned once and gave me the phone number for a lawyer who would handle everything. "I have to vanish," Jo said. "I won't be contacting you again. But good luck. I mean great luck. I hope the church idea works out."

"Me too," I told him. "Me too."

That lawyer told me he had purchased an earthquake damaged middle school on Highland Boulevard in Los Angeles. My first job was to move into a hotel nearby and to meet with the architects and civil engineers. We planned how to tear the old school down and how to build an earthquake-proof church in its place.

I listened to the architect drone on about column styles and history. We sat in one of the conference rooms of my hotel. Bland walls and white table cloths, a setting of coffee and tea by the door.

The architect tapped his pen to get my attention. "What will be your color theme?" he asked.

Jo said I wouldn't blow up, and how I was surrounded by men in yellow robes. "Yellow," I said. "A pale lemon yellow. A soft springtime yellow. The yellow of a summer sun."

"Yellow 615," he said, and wrote in his notebook.

"Yeah," I said. Of course, I had no idea what the 615 meant. "Yellow 615." I thought that might make a good answer to a crossword clue.

After that, others showed up who also believed a church was necessary and who believed in what Jo Bailey stood for. Unlike the Defoe Scallody gang, these men were thoughtful and honest. I thought I might resent help, but the scale of the undertaking soon convinced me to accept a few of the best of them into the fold. Six others joined me as priests and founders. Six, like the six other men who, with me, had joined Defoe Scallody's gang.

So I came eventually to sit in my office on the third floor of an actual new church. My wide, wood framed window overlooks the small cemetery out back with its seven sad graves. Seven graves like there were seven men in Scallody's gang. Seven and seven, I think, the name of a drink and I wish I could have one, but I no longer drink.

Pale yellow curtains lent a summer warm glow to my room despite clouds and grey rain outside. A chess game unstarted on my desk next to a photo of Father Desmond. I can hear the rain start again, heavy. The sound of water gurgling down the rain spouts. I write how I came to sit where I do. I write how I betrayed then befriended Jo Bailey. I write for you Joy, this, my confession, and I ask you to forgive me.

Events of 1987-1998
Dustin Willowsmith

Reporter for the San Francisco Examiner, Reconstructed notes of several stories about Jo Bailey

Late that afternoon I visited the Cabbage Valley Retirement Center. Chef Gibions had not arrived yet so I walked the grounds. One old man seemed to eye me suspiciously so I walked over to him. "Hi," I said. "I'm Dustin Willowsmith. Used to be a reporter following Jo Bailey, but I'm presently writing a cookbook."

The old man smiled. "Did you say Jo Bailey?"

I sat on the brick planter next to him. "Yes I did. Does that name mean something to you?"

He reached out an astonishingly wrinkled hand to shake mine. "Tony Waxman," he said.

Tony sat in a wheelchair on an expansive area of brick, shaded by huge mature oak trees. A grey and red striped blanket covered his lap despite the warm day.

"I was in charge that afternoon," He said. "I was a policeman then and I was there the day Jo Bailey's mother was shot."

I gazed at Tony. He appeared sincere. He seemed much sharper than the typical old man. I wondered why he was in a retirement home but didn't ask. His hair was completely white, not grey. Even the few chest hairs I could glimpse below his neck in his open shirt collar were pure white too. White hairs against his sky blue shirt.

Tony rolled his wheelchair, the manual kind, into a patch of shade. I followed and sat on the edge of a another wide planter box; purple wisteria, red tulips, and yellow daisies.

Tony continued. "I had gone out to the street to tell the officers to keep an eye peeled for Jo. But Jo snookered me. I hadn't seen him coming. I found him in the kitchen standing stock still like a small statue. He stood there and stared at his mother."

Tony's voice was deep and mellow. "Jo's mother," he continued. "Lay on her back with a small pool of blood around her head. And I swear, Jo asked me if that was a halo."

Tony opened a canvas bag slung on the side of his wheelchair and pulled out a plastic bottle of water. He drank and offered me the bottle. I shook my head. I wanted to hear more.

Tony smacked his lips. I could see he was watching me. He kept the bottle on his lap and continued, "Jo's mother, you see, had been shot once in the chest and once between her eyes. That second hole looked like that spot worn by Indian women, low on their forehead, above the eyes, dead center." Tony touched his forehead to show where the shot had been and left a wet spot that glistened there.

"Joe said to me, 'I'm sorry I couldn't save her,' and turned to run, but I put a firm hand on his shoulder. I led him to the front porch and told him to wait there."

"Then the oddest thing happened. I felt Jo go rigid," Tony paused to carefully shift his wheelchair to the left in order to escape the sun slowly overtaking him from shadow's edge. "Naturally I thought Jo was afraid, but then he fell out from under my hand to the cement porch and began to shake. I thought Jo was having an epileptic seizure." Tony rubbed his forehead with the back of his hand like he was rubbing the echo of a wound off.

"The other officers saw me trying to shove my baton into Jo's mouth to keep him from biting his tongue." Tony chuckled then coughed. "They thought I was beating the boy and were sure surprised when they found out Jo was having a seizure. They ribbed me about that for months after.

"Jo woke up later in my office. 'I couldn't save her,' is what Jo said to me when he woke up. Course not, I told him. be quiet for a while so I can finish my report. Yeah, I said, something like that.

"Emma, I think that was her name —with children's services— came in and walked all the way into the room and stood right in front of Jo. She told him he was a 'foster child' and would be placed into a 'foster home.' She said her words like that. She made no bones about pretense.

"I couldn't save her, Jo said to her then. Emma acted like she didn't hear him. She told him, she was sure he'll do fine."

I interrupted Tony, "Didn't you find that unusual? Him saying he couldn't save his mother?"

Tony rubbed his chin. "Don't know. Kids say all sorts of odd things when their folks are killed. I can't swear that's what he said, but that's what I remember."

"Please continue."

"That's about all. Emma led Jo out and into her car. And that was the last I saw or heard of him."

I stared at him for a moment, considering Jo's remark. Then I asked, "Do you know who killed his mother?"

"Off the record?"

"You're not a policeman any more are you?"

"Oh, yeah." He sounded sad. "Okay then. Dr. Scallody's son, that's who killed her. I don't know the boy's name. Anyway, after the lawsuit, Dr. Scallody hanged himself in his front room. His son found him. He, that's right, his name was Defoe —odd name for a boy— he was really more a young man. Defoe Scallody. Yes. He blamed the Bailey's I guess, for his dad losing everything and hanging himself. Defoe had motive. We found out he owned a pistol, but could never get enough evidence to tie him to the murder."

"But why was Jo made a foster kid. Why wasn't he sent to live with his Dad in Charleston?"

Tony leaned forward and crossed his hands in his lap again. "I don't know. Never crossed my mind that child services could make a mistake. Goes to show you, maybe they can."

I thanked Tony and left him there in his wheelchair under the shade of summer oak trees on that wide brick patio surrounded by blooming flowers, his hands folded on the blanket over his lap and his eyes drooping as if he were about to take a nap.

At home that evening I opened a bottle of Pentfolds 2005 St. Henri Shiraz from Australia. An expensive wine I had been saving for a special occasion. While I let the bottle breathe, I stood at my living room window and watched the city lights twinkle. My third floor apartment provided enough of a downtown view to be special, but not so spectacular to demand a high rent. I touched the glass with my open palm and felt the outside warmth. I wondered about death and dimensions and decided I couldn't do a heck of a lot about either. For some reason then, I reminded myself of that comedy, "A Funny Thing Happened On The Way To The Forum." Miles Gloriosus, the grand Roman soldier spoke of a promised wife who died, "Poor thing. She probably flew too near my flame."

Well that's how I felt that evening. Like I'd flown too near a flame. I felt singed but alive. I didn't tumble back to earth, my wings burned. I had escaped with a near miss. My salvation was my anticlimax.

I walked back to the kitchen and poured myself a glass of the wine. One sip, and I knew I had saved that bottle for a good reason. I carried the glass back to the living room window and tinked the rim against the glass in a toast. "To Jo," I said. "To Joy and the Church."

I took a sip and thought about the future. I tinked the window again and said, "To Jo's mom, so long ago shot to death in her kitchen."

My computer beeped. I glanced over at the screen. A reply from Joy had arrived. She had received my latest report from Concord.

I laughed then. I couldn't figure out why. But I found my whole situation funny. Witness yes, participant maybe. I recalled Greg my former editor then, and tapped the window one more time. "To Bobby Fisher," I said and chuckled, strangely truly happy.

About The Author

Bryan Costales is an American Author born Chicago, Illinois and raised in Concord, California. His vocations have ranged from news photographer, to window designer, to display manager, to art director for motion pictures, to Unix system administrator, to software engineer. His writing career began with a modest technical book called "C from A to Z." Since then he has written several more technical books culminating in "sendmail" (the bat book) for O'Reilly Media. He has professionally published a few short stories. He studied with the San Francisco Writing Salon, the San Francisco Writer's Grotto, and the Grape Writing Method. This book is his first novel.

Bryan currently lives in the Great Northwest with his lovely wife Terry and his nimble dog Gypsy who cannot yet jump through a hoop.

www.ingramcontent.com/pod-product-compliance
Lightning Source LLC
Chambersburg PA
CBHW050426260626
47156CB00003B/1171